INVASIVE SPECIES

FREAKY FLORIDA BOOK 2

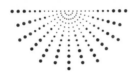

WARD PARKER

MAD MANGROVE MEDIA

MAN VS. REPTILE

It takes a special kind of man to jump into a mosquito-infested swamp at night to tackle a ten-foot snake. In Shugg Spencer's case, it was a man in dire need of money.

The moment he caught sight of the python in the spotlight he shined from the cab of his truck in Florida's Everglades, Shugg stopped and jumped out. He slid down the bank of the levee and plunged waist-deep into the lukewarm water and mud of the swamp without hesitation. Burmese pythons aren't particularly skittish, but once they figure out you're coming after them, they'll make themselves scarce. And this one, illuminated by his headlamp with its head rising from the water a good two feet, flickered its tongue to catch his scent, then promptly ducked under the water.

That was why Shugg didn't just shoot the damn snakes like some of the lazier bounty hunters did. If you shoot them and they go off to die somewhere hidden, you can't bring them in and get your money. The real pros, like himself, caught them by hand and dispatched them with a humane pointblank shot to the head from a bolt gun.

That is assuming you could catch them. And they didn't catch you first.

Shugg dove atop the last place he had seen the snake and landed on its thick, muscular middle section. He grabbed it and ducked as the head came at him. Pythons don't have venom, but they sure do have teeth as he had discovered the hard way in the past. Stymied from biting him, the snake wrenched free and began climbing up a young buttonwood tree.

Dang, he had to get it out of there fast.

Shugg grabbed it again and wrestled it out of the branches before it could fasten itself to them.

Then the snake fell on him.

As the snake was wrapping around his shoulders, Shugg tried to grab it right behind its oblong head. If he could manage that without being bitten, and before he was crushed and asphyxiated, he would win.

There, he had it in his right hand, right behind the jaws. The snake seemed resigned to its loss. It coiled itself around his left arm and didn't squeeze him as much as other species of constrictors would have. That was typical of the twenty-four Burmese pythons he had caught over the last year. He just needed to wade to dry land and "humanely euthanize" it as the South Florida Water Management District officials would say— the folks who paid him $8.50 per hour plus a by-the-foot bonus.

Shugg didn't have any qualms about killing critters. A life-time living in the swamps and poaching gators made it easy. He and his little brother Bugg had learned from their daddy how to skin gators before they learned to walk.

Catching Burmese pythons was actually doing a good deed.

The invasive species, released into the wild by exotic pet owners and the havoc created by Hurricane Andrew, had destroyed the ecosystem of the Everglades. These apex predators multiplied like crazy and ate almost every critter that lived there, even gators. Shugg hadn't seen any rabbits or raccoons for years.

He knew that he and the other python hunters were barely making a dent in the python population. But the important thing was making some extra cash. After all, he was on the hook for two alimony payments. Never mind that he hadn't paid Melinda or Peggy Sue a dime for over a year, but his third wife liked to shop, and his money woes weighed heavily on him like the fifty pounds or so of snake he carried out of the swamp.

Just as he was climbing the grassy embankment to the road, clouds of mosquitoes swirling around him, something caught his eye several yards to his right. Some creature was moving through the weeds. In the darkness he couldn't tell what it was. It was at least a few feet long, had a long tail, and looked reptilian. It could be a baby gator. No, it had the wrong shape.

It must be an iguana, another of Florida's invasive species that was multiplying out of control. But were iguanas active at night? Maybe it was a monitor lizard, another less-common invasive species. Whatever it was, something was very unusual about this critter.

Shugg still had the giant snake wrapped around him and his hand firmly held its neck. If he brought the snake to his truck and euthanized it, the strange critter would be gone by the time he returned to this spot. Something deep in his mercenary soul told him this new critter might be worth some money.

He crept closer along the slope to where the weeds were moving and shined his headlamp at the spot. He got another glimpse of the tail. It was covered with spikes and the end was shaped like an arrowhead. This critter looked more like a dinosaur than an iguana.

The weeds rustled and the creature walked into view.

It looked just like . . . a dragon.

What kind of freaking lizard is this? he wondered.

Colored a dark brown-green, its sinuous body was covered in rough scales. A muscular body moved on four legs with long claws and bat-like wings sprouted from its back. The tail whipped back and forth in agitation. The head, on the end of a long, graceful neck, had a small horn at the end of its nose and two larger ones on the top of its head. It flapped its wings, trying to flee, but didn't leave the ground. One wing appeared to be damaged. It backed away from him and his offending headlamp.

Then flames shot out from its mouth, burning a patch of weeds.

It *was* a freaking dragon, a baby.

Dragons weren't supposed to exist. So this one could be worth millions of dollars. And he would become famous as the Discoverer of Dragons.

He wasn't sure if he should take a selfie—that would be kind of cool, him with a python *and* a dragon. But he decided to make sure the creature didn't escape first.

Now he wished he had both hands free and didn't have a fifty-plus-pound, increasingly restless, burden wrapped around his left arm. Should he ditch the snake?

He quickly calculated that the snake, at about ten feet long, would net him at least $200, not counting the hourly wage. The dragon, though, was priceless, if he could figure out how to monetize it.

Why not keep both critters?

He transferred the snake's head to his left hand. With his left arm inside the enormous brown, shiny coil of the python, that hand was useless. With his newly freed right hand, he pulled from his back pocket a canvas sack that he used to carry smaller pythons when he found more than one. He shook it open and moved closer to the dragon. Working one-handed, he had to do this just right.

The dragon began backing away. Holding onto the sack's drawstring, which was about twenty feet long, he tossed the sack just behind the dragon and yanked the string, pulling the bag back toward him into the dragon's path. He couldn't get the opening around the reptile, as it flailed in panic, emitting spurts of flame that singed the bag. But Shugg did manage to tangle its two right legs and wing inside the bag.

This was too crazy, he had to get a photo. He wrapped the bag's string around his belt and withdrew his phone from his shirt pocket. He took a bunch of photos of the dragon struggling with the sack, then turned and got a nice selfie of his face and the dragon. He posted them on social media with only a cryptic message typed with his thumb:

Found real dragon in Everglades.

He had to get the snake in a photo, too. It would be so viral. He adjusted the position of the phone and twisted his body, trying to get his face, the snake, and the dragon in the same shot.

The dragon was terrified of Shugg and of the other reptilian species being carried by him. And the snake became agitated by the unfamiliar reptilian creature that it normally would have eaten, if the prey hadn't been spouting flames, as well as by his human captor moving and twisting erratically. As for Shugg, he was exceedingly amped up by the whole experience but getting frustrated trying to compose the ultimate viral, man-vs.-exotic-reptiles photo.

THE CRAZY MIXED SCENTS—OF human skin plus the strange fiery reptile plus the burning canvas sack plus reptilian fear plus human adrenaline—were too much for the snake to handle.

The Burmese python eased its grip on the human's arm and managed to slip its coils around the human's neck. And it squeezed with every ounce of strength it had.

SHUGG QUICKLY CAME to the conclusion that he should have let the damn snake go when he'd had the chance. The sudden lack of oxygen to the brain helped clarify this fact. He tried forcing his fingers between his neck and the snake's coils, but the snake's grip was too tight. He tried to pry it off by yanking its head, but it managed to slip its head from his hand and bite it.

And soon, he didn't have the chance to do anything at all.

2

FOUND FRIEND

Missy Mindle was deep in Everglades National Park and she was lost. She was also being harassed by a mosquito trapped in her car. Not just any mosquito, an Everglades mosquito. Which is like comparing a house cat to a hyena.

During the day, if you're in direct sunshine, you won't be bothered by Everglades mosquitos. But beneath the shadow of a tree, even on the brightest hour of the day, you may as well offer a pint of blood and save yourself the hundreds of pin pricks. Missy had made the mistake of opening her window a crack near a tree and now was paying the price as the insect dive-bombed her and dodged her every attempt to swat it.

She drove slowly along a dirt road atop a levee through prairie wetlands dotted with islands of scraggly trees. There was no shade here, but try telling that to the mosquito in her car. She was looking for pennyroyal growing in the wild, which she needed for certain magick potions. Pennyroyal was not the kind of herb you wanted to buy in the store. If you looked hard enough you could find it sold live; otherwise, it was offered dried, half-stale, and less potent than the fresh stuff. Freshly picked from the wild was the most powerful version.

You could say Missy was a witch. It wasn't her profession—which was a home-health nurse—but it was her calling. It had begun simply as a hobby, but in time it kindled dormant powers that she'd had since birth. Because she was an orphan, she'd never had anyone to ask from where the powers had originated. In fact, her adoptive parents refused to talk about witchcraft and forbade her from learning about it. They never explained why.

Nevertheless, beginning when she was in college she had dabbled in Wicca and in what she called Florida Cracker Folk Magick. Both were the kinds of witchcraft that used elements of the earth to draw out the earth's power. But she also had hard-to-understand powers within her which were strengthened by the craft of magick and vice versa. She could perform actions with telekinetic energy simply by concentrating her mind, but her abilities were enhanced by spells that used elements of the earth.

That included fresh, natural ingredients like pennyroyal. Which was why she was lost. She had been driving on a main visitor road early in the morning, looking for the cutoff that led to a trail head. But she mistakenly turned onto a dirt road that had a gate left open. The road didn't appear on any map apps. It felt as if it was circling back to the main road, so she kept rolling slowly forward, because the road was too narrow to turn around and had no shoulder. Her ancient Toyota Corolla definitely could not handle off-road expeditions.

The mosquito pricked the back of her neck. She slapped herself, but her hand came back empty. She had yet to learn spells that could kill a mosquito in your car.

She was just beginning to go around a bend when she slammed on her brakes.

A canvas sack lay in the middle of the road. The sack was squirming. Something was trapped partially inside. A dark, brown-green lizard of some sort struggled to free itself of the canvas, whipping a long tail and rolling around in the dirt. It appeared to be a large iguana.

She felt sorry for the lizard and wanted to help it. But there was no way she was going to handle the thing. She reached into her cluttered back seat and pulled out a plastic clothes hanger.

Getting out of the car, she approached the creature warily. It turned its head, protruding from a hole in the sack, toward her. The hole was burned around its edges.

Its head didn't look like an iguana's. Mature green iguanas have a soft, spiky-looking crest running from their neck to the base of their tail. But not horns on their head or on their nose. And this lizard's nostrils were larger and surrounded by cartilage.

Its limbs, that weren't trapped in the sack, looked alligator-like with their hard, scale armor. But the tail had a flared triangular tip that she'd never seen before on an alligator or American crocodile. This lizard looked more like a dinosaur.

She got closer and the creature retreated, hobbled by the sack. But it didn't attempt to flee outright. It stared at her with its horizontally slitted pupils as if it wasn't scared of humans, just wary.

She circled around it to get a better look at the parts that weren't inside the sack.

What she saw made her gasp.

It had wings. Folded to its body were two large skin-covered wings like a pterodactyl's.

She didn't know of any contemporary member of the lizard

family like this. Was it some undiscovered species that secretly lived in the Everglades?

She reached toward it with the hanger to help free it from the sack. It squeaked in alarm.

And belched flames.

She jumped back.

This was a dragon. A baby dragon or a miniature, Shetland-pony version of a dragon.

With its subtropical climate, South Florida, was teeming with species that didn't belong here, like iguanas and other reptiles. But a dragon? Where in the world did it come from? Or was it actually native to Florida?

She was so astounded she didn't even think to take a picture of it. She continued her attempt to hook the hanger on the canvas and pull the sack off. And for some reason it now allowed her to do it. When she finally snagged the sack and lifted it around the fragile wings, the dragon did the rest of the work and extricated itself. It was about three and a half to four feet long, including the tail.

It flapped its wings, but didn't go anywhere. One of the wings appeared to be broken.

"It's okay," she said to it in a soothing voice. "I'll help you. I'll get your wing fixed."

It lifted its head and sniffed the air, turning in a circle, looking to the sky and sniffing more. It crouched cat-like, almost touching the ground with its chest, looking up, and searching the sky.

"What are you afraid of, little one?"

She could forget about collecting any pennyroyal. She needed to get medical attention for the dragon, but didn't feel it was wise to take it to a veterinarian. After all, she understood the importance of keeping secret the existence of supernatural creatures.

She could perform rudimentary care, but she didn't have the skills to correctly set the broken wing. She would have to request the services of Dr. Hyde. Her employer, Acceptance Home Care, kept Dr. Hyde on retainer to make house calls for their clients: elderly supernatural and mythical creatures, such as vampires, werewolves and other shifters, trolls, ogres—you name it. There were a surprising number of them in Florida.

Her job as a home-health nurse was to provide basic care for their clients who, naturally, couldn't show up at a hospital or doctor's office. When they needed more advanced care than she could provide—when their supernatural healing abilities weren't enough—she called in Dr. Hyde. She didn't know if he also handled non-humanoid monsters, but at least he was open-minded and could be trusted.

But how would she get the dragon home? Would it ever allow her to pick it up?

She opened the door to her car in order to search for a treat to tempt the dragon into her car. No, it wouldn't want breath mints, she thought, tossing the tin to the floor. She found an empty cup among the litter in her back seat and filled it from her water bottle.

She sensed movement behind her, then something brushed against her leg.

The dragon jumped into the car and climbed into the passenger seat just like a dog.

"Good dragon," she said, not knowing what else to say.

She placed the cup of water on the console next to the seat. The dragon sniffed it, then began to lap it up, its head almost too big to fit into the cup. She slipped into the driver's seat, carefully without startling the dragon, and started the engine. Since she couldn't turn around, and didn't want to back up for miles on the narrow dirt road, Missy continued driving forward until either the road joined another, or she could find a place to turn around.

That's when the sky split open.

No, it wasn't a thunderstorm, though Florida does have some spectacular ones, particularly over the wetlands of the Everglades. In this case, the sky remained perfectly sunny and blue, yet a deafening crack of thunder rocked the car. A circular black shape appeared directly overhead, like a hole in the sky. Then it extended as a perfectly straight black band that stretched until it touched the horizon in both the east and west. The band widened as if the earth's atmosphere were opening up.

A dark funnel cloud descended in a straight vertical line from the crack in the sky, an impossibly tall tornado that went from the heavens to the earth. When it touched down in the wetlands a few miles to the west, it turned into a waterspout, spinning about in random directions and breaking off from the tall funnel cloud. As quickly as it all had begun, the remaining funnel cloud withdrew into the crack in the atmosphere and the black band across the sky closed, leaving no trace.

All that was left was the seemingly ordinary waterspout wandering across the grassy wetlands. It hit a hammock, a small island of trees, and dissipated. Missy breathed a sigh of relief and pushed her car a little faster until it started shaking on the rough dirt road.

Something was wrong.

She felt watched. She looked in the rearview mirror then scanned the landscape around her car. Nothing was around except for a flock of ibis. The mosquitoes didn't count. There were surely other wild creatures watching her car, hidden, but this feeling was different. It was an intelligent being that watched her. A malevolent one. She just knew it.

A large shadow of indeterminate shape glided across the sea of grass. It wasn't created by a cloud and there was nothing else in the sky that could have caused it. The shadow was coming at a rapid speed right toward her.

The dragon made a high-pitched, raspy cry that was surprisingly loud for its size.

She had to cast a barrier spell immediately. It wasn't the strongest form of protection, but it was the easiest and quickest to cast.

Stopping the car, she slammed the gear into Park and focused on creating a barrier shield, a dome of power enclosing the entire car and its living cargo.

She chanted the magick words. The words themselves were meaningless for this spell, but they were like a mantra guiding her mind, tapping into her own powers, and funneling those from the earth. She wove together the barrier with her mind and felt it form, surrounding her, and then growing in density and strength.

The shadow swooped in, swallowing the car. It blocked all light.

A tremendous force hit the protective dome, sending her brain reeling. The dragon screamed again. The darkness was so thick, so complete, she couldn't see anything, even the screen of her watch.

Missy concentrated harder, trying to maintain the spell as the entity pounded against the shield—hundreds of blows from every angle. The car shook with each impact. She reached deep inside herself and tried to find more energy to maintain the shield and make it stronger. The dragon whimpered.

Pairs of glowing red eyes appeared in the windshield and

the windows. Though there were multiple pairs, she sensed a single consciousness. It studied the occupants of the car. She felt it trying to probe her mind, somehow getting through the shield. She added another layer of protection and the probing ceased.

Suddenly, the darkness was gone. The sun shined and the blue sky was above them again. There was no shadow in sight. Everything was normal, except her car radio had turned on by itself. A Cuban merengue tune blasted from a Miami station.

She breathed a big sigh of relief.

The dragon looked up at her. She swore she saw affection in its eyes. But then it opened its jaws and she flinched, fearing fire would come out.

What came out instead were words:

"Girl, you've got some badass power!"

"I BEG YOUR PARDON?" Missy asked the dragon that was sitting on her passenger seat. Reptiles weren't supposed to talk.

"I said you have some serious power," the dragon replied, looking her in the eyes. It had a Southern accent. "Was my choice of words a little too salty for you?"

"No, I'm just not used to dragons that talk. Actually, I'm not used to dragons at all."

"Well, I'm not used to humans. But my mother is. She was hatched and raised by a human farmer in Jensen Beach back in the 1890s. He taught her to speak English and she taught me when I was just a baby. Dragons have always been able to speak human languages, though we generally try to avoid coming into contact with y'all."

"I would ask why, but I'm still trying to process having a dragon in my car."

"Why we speak human, or why we try to avoid you?"

"Both, I guess," Missy said.

"If you know your dragon history, you'd recall that our two species usually fight one another. But dragons are good at manipulating humans, especially if we know your languages."

The dirt road had finally widened enough for Missy to turn the car around. She headed back the way she had come, hoping that no one had locked the gate behind her. It felt like she'd been on this road for eons, but it had probably only been an hour or so.

"Are you a male dragon or female dragon?" Missy asked. "No offense, but I don't really know how to—"

"I'm a male. My name is Ronnie, by the way."

"I'm Missy. Wait, are you really expecting me to believe that a dragon is named Ronnie?"

"Yeah, I told you my mom grew up in Florida. She was a big fan of Florida-boy Ronnie Van Zant of the band Lynyrd Skynyrd."

"Oh, of course. Why didn't I think of that?"

"I want to thank you for saving my life back there," the dragon named Ronnie said. "And I don't only mean freeing me from that sack."

"What was that *thing* that attacked us?"

"It was me that it wanted. It had been chasing me and I crossed over and ended up here in Florida. I didn't think it knew I came here and would come after me."

"I don't understand," Missy said, trying to keep their speed as fast as possible without her car shaking apart on the rough road. "What exactly is that thing and where did you come from?"

"I don't know exactly what that thing is, except that it's very powerful and very evil and I worry that it got my mother. She has battled it before. She said it's our heritage and duty as dragons to fight it and keep it from invading Florida and the rest of the world. For some reason, it really has a problem with me. But I've never done anything to tick it off."

"How did you get separated from your mother?"

"She sent me through the gateway to save me. I thought she would come right behind me. But she didn't show up. She was trying to stop the evil entity."

"Don't worry, I'm sure she's okay. Now, you still haven't told me where you came from."

"We were taking refuge in another world. I can't tell you any more than that. We dragons are forbidden to give information about it to humans. Your ancestors who tried to make us extinct are the reason we began to escape there in the first place."

"But why Florida?"

"I was born in Florida and so was my mother. We spend a lot of time here. Dragons used to live here all the time. The Everglades is a great place to hang out and hunt without being noticed. And Florida has always been like a border crossing between many worlds."

"Well, it's known as the gateway to Latin America and, I guess, to New York," Missy said. "Your accent doesn't place you from either region."

The dragon laughed. It sounded a bit like a sneeze. "It's also a gateway for animal migrations, ocean currents, climates. And other planes of existence."

"You're a smart dragon for a baby."

"I'm not a baby," Ronnie said, annoyed. "I'm almost an adult. I just happen to be small for my age."

"And what age would that be?"

"I'll be eighty next month. And even when I'm all grown up, I won't be gigantic. I come from a line of small dragons. It's easier to hide when you're small."

They finally arrived at the main, paved road and the gate was still open. Missy pulled out and headed toward the national park entrance and, eventually, the highway home.

"It's very dangerous for you to help me," Ronnie said.

"We need to get your wing fixed," she said.

"I'm serious. You could be destroyed along with me."

"Let's not think about that now. How did you break your wing?"

"Don't ask."

"No, really."

"A house cat, okay? In a backyard in Homestead. Those evil beasts are true invasive species, if you ask me."

"Then I need to prepare you for what you're going to meet at my home."

3

BAD BLOOD

"I told you we shouldn't have flown commercial," Oleg Kazmirov muttered to his traveling companion, Leonard Schwartz, as the two elderly vampires were led from the Miami International Airport Customs checkpoint into a nearby screening room.

"Charter flights are so expensive," Schwartz said.

No self-respecting vampire would fly commercial, let alone coach, Oleg thought. A bit of a snob, he had once been a cavalry officer under Catherine the Great and his family had belonged to the minor aristocracy.

The obese Customs and Border Protection agent with a shaved head tossed his suitcase atop a table. He opened it and looked for secret compartments, then rummaged through Oleg's unwashed clothing. He removed Oleg's riding crop and studied it with a confused expression. Then a light clicked on beneath his heavily lidded eyes. He looked at Oleg with a smirk.

"Giddy up, baby," the agent said, smacking the crop against his own butt.

Oleg gritted his teeth and faked a grin (making sure his fangs were still retracted despite his anger). How long was this idiot going to draw this out?

The idiot gestured for Oleg to follow him to a small, windowless room with boxes piled in the corner. He told him to take a seat at the table that dominated the room.

Oleg saw Schwartz pass by the open doorway, led by another agent down the hall.

Why did Oleg allow his friend to cheap out on the transportation? It wasn't as if they weren't willing to spend money. They booked the high-end suite at the resort in Punta Cana and spent a small fortune on a different bevy of young chicas every night. It was the perfect Guy Getaway, particularly for guys who happened to be vampires and knew how to feed discretely. Well, it had been perfect until they had to go through Customs like the everyday riffraff.

The door opened and a different man entered. He wasn't wearing a uniform. Navy-blue slacks, white dress shirt, narrow Navy tie. A Homeland Security badge clipped on his shirt pocket. He was young with a black beard and suspicious eyes.

"I'm Agent Alvarez," he said.

"Am I under arrest?" Oleg asked.

"No, and you're not suspected of any crime."

"I am a naturalized citizen of this country," Oleg said.

"Your citizenship is not in question," Alvarez said, glancing at Oleg's passport which had been confiscated at the checkpoint. "Your birthdate says 1983. You, uh, look a bit older than that."

When you're a centuries-old vampire in the modern world, you have to resort to a lot of forged paperwork. He obviously couldn't use his actual 1743 birthdate. After he received his forged birth certificate, he had discovered that some forgers were stupider than others.

"I served in the military in Russia," Oleg said. "It aged me considerably."

"I see. Now tell me again why you and Mr. Schwartz were visiting the Dominican Republic. Based on your complexion, you obviously didn't go there to soak in the sunshine."

"The culture?"

"Wasn't it the girls? Your friend was quick to brag about it to the Customs officer."

"He's proud of being a ladies' man."

"Of soliciting prostitutes?"

Oleg remained silent.

"We need to search your phone. And we don't need a warrant to do it. May I have your phone, please?"

"I don't have one."

"You don't have a phone?"

"I don't like those silly gadgets. I'm an old-fashioned guy." It was true.

Alvarez stared at him with disbelief, then glanced at his notes which probably reported on the results of when Oleg and Schwartz were searched.

"Can you tell me why your friend had vials of blood in his suitcase?"

No, he couldn't. Oleg couldn't explain that the vials contained werewolf blood, which was like Viagra for vampires. Though vampires were immortal, if they happened to have been elderly humans when they were turned into vampires, they spent the rest of eternity as elderly vampires. And, sometimes, an old guy needed a little help when it came to bedroom matters. Schwartz did, that is, not himself. Not often, at least. In any event, it was stupid for Schwartz to have brought it back into the country. He should have dumped the leftover vials before they left Punta Cana.

"Something to do with diabetes?" Oleg knew he didn't sound very convincing.

Alvarez gave a disgusted sigh and stood. "You know, we don't have to let you back into the country."

"What did I do wrong?"

"I don't know. I just know I don't like you," Alvarez said, leaving the room and closing the door.

Oleg sat beneath the buzzing fluorescent lighting. He glanced at his watch which they hadn't taken from him. It was past dawn, so he wouldn't be able to leave the airport and go outside anyway. He crossed his arms on the table and rested his head upon them, closing his eyes. He dozed off and dreamed of leading his regiment of hussars in a battlefield charge, back when he was mortal but feared nothing and never was subjected to disrespect.

Hours later, the door opened and an unfamiliar CBP agent, a young woman, came in.

"Mr. Kazmirov?"

He nodded.

"You're free to go. Your possessions are on the table by the exit."

Oleg checked his watch. There were only a few hours before dusk to kill if he could find an area of the airport that didn't have windows. Then they could leave the airport and drive home. Oleg knew there were extremely wealthy vampires who could travel at any time of day using their private jets and limousines with darkened windows. But, no, he would be heading back to Jellyfish Beach in Schwartz's grimy old Lexus that was currently sitting in the long-term parking garage.

There was a problem, however. When Oleg collected his suitcase and passport, he didn't see Schwartz anywhere.

"Excuse me," he flagged down the agent who had released him. "Where is my friend, Leonard Schwartz?"

She looked away uncomfortably. "He's been detained for further questioning."

"But I can't leave without him."

"He's not here anymore. They sent him to another facility."

"But where?"

"I'm not allowed to say."

"That is unacceptable," Oleg said with all the upper-class indignation he could muster.

The agent frowned, her patience nearing its end. "Please leave now or you'll be arrested."

Oleg left the hidden lair of the CBP and reentered the noisy terminal. Wheeling his bag after him, he wandered disconsolately into a corridor of retail and food service where there were no outside windows. The area was clogged with humans. Hundreds of fresh meals within arm's length wandering around like livestock, oblivious to the predator in their midst.

But he ignored his hunger and did the only thing he could think to do: call his vampire leader—Agnes, the president of the Squid Tower Homeowners Association.

"Hi Agnes, it's Oleg Kazmirov. Sorry to bother you. We have a problem: Schwartz has been detained by Homeland Security. Oh, and I need a ride home from the airport."

SCHWARTZ COULDN'T BELIEVE he was handcuffed and sitting in a disgusting holding cell in the Miami-Dade Police airport substation. He hadn't even realized such a facility existed here in the airport. That this shiny airport with gift shops selling cheesy T-shirts and food courts with Mongolian woks and Cuban sandwiches had a seedy underbelly of jail cells was hard to process.

As was the fact that he was totally screwed. He needed to call his lawyer, but the cops hadn't allowed him to. Jacob wasn't a criminal lawyer, though. He merely handled the endless series of lawsuits that Schwartz filed against Jellyfish Beach and anything or anyone else who annoyed him. The great thing about Jacob is that while he himself had aged (tremendously) over the forty-some-odd years that Schwartz had retained him, he never asked why Schwartz hadn't aged too. Or died, for that matter.

The cell stank of urine and unwashed bodies. Schwartz's vampire senses made the smell that much more unbearable. With his preternatural strength, he probably could break the chain of the handcuffs, though he wasn't sure if he could defeat the lock on the steel door of the cell. However, there were too many witnesses. It was a really bad idea to let normal humans know that you're a supernatural creature.

"I don't care about your outdated system," a loud voice boomed from out in the office area of the station. "I have orders straight from D.C."

A large man with a stubble haircut wearing a navy-blue jacket with an ICE logo on the back of it was speaking with the officer behind the counter.

"We just brought him down here and haven't even booked him yet," the officer said.

"That makes it even better," the large man said. "The chain of custody will be that much simpler."

More conversation ensued that Schwartz couldn't hear,

followed by mutual laughter. Then the Miami-Dade Police officer appeared, unlocking the holding cell.

"C'mon, old man. You're going on a ride with ICE."

Immigration and Customs Enforcement. They're the ones who bust undocumented immigrants and smugglers. Schwartz wondered, what did they want with him?

The officer removed the handcuffs and the ICE agent, who had a bushy black mustache and dead eyes, replaced them with his own set. Without saying a word, he led Schwartz out of the police substation and through a warren of subterranean hallways to a small parking lot outside the terminal. He pushed him into the back seat of a black SUV.

Soon, they were speeding along a highway. It was still dark out, but only a couple of hours remained before dawn. Schwartz hoped they reached their destination before that. Dying from sunlight in the back of a cop car was not the way he'd want to end his eternal life.

"Hey, what's your name?" Schwartz asked, trying to ingratiate himself with the agent. Schwartz had never been very good at that. "I'm Leonard."

The agent's eyes appeared in the rearview mirror. "Bill Jaffe," he said. "Formerly with ICE."

"Formerly? But you're wearing the ICE jacket."

"I'm a freelancer now."

"Where are we going?"

"To a very special facility. For very special individuals like you."

4

NEW MEMBER OF THE FAMILY

Brenda and Bubba were not amused. Missy's two gray
tabbies didn't bother showing the least bit of hospi-
tality when they greeted their new houseguest. Brenda,
atop a bookcase in the living room, and Bubba, balancing on the
back of a chair, arched their backs and hissed in unison when
they saw the dragon amble into their house behind Missy.

"Brenda and Bubba, meet Ronnie," Missy said.

"Nice welcoming committee," Ronnie said. "And *I'm* the
cold-blooded one?"

Bubba growled.

"Let's make sure there's no bloodshed. For your own safety,
I'm going to have to keep you where the cats can't get to you."

"Oh, I can defend myself," Ronnie said, bristling. "No cat is
going to ambush me again."

"That's what I'm worried about. I don't want you to
barbecue my cats. They're my children. Got that?"

"Got it."

"Would you prefer to be kept in the guest bedroom, with air conditioning, or out in the garage?"

"Does 'kept' mean imprisoned?"

"For your own protection."

"I'd prefer the garage. I'm not an indoor dragon. Does it have a window for ventilation?"

"It does. Do you, um, use a litter box? Or—"

"I'll go outdoors to take care of business."

"Let's go out there now and set you up before the cats go feral on us. Follow me."

She led the way to her small laundry room near the kitchen and opened a door to the garage.

"I hope you don't mind all the junk out here. I haven't had room to park my car in here for years."

Ronnie followed her down a step onto the concrete floor of the garage. The garage door was closed but had a row of small windows that let in some light. A window on the side wall also helped with illumination. She flicked a switch on the wall and turned on fluorescent lights on the ceiling.

"Humans sure like their stuff," Ronnie said.

Since she had an older house from the 1940s, it was only a one-car garage. And she had managed to fill it with a lawn-mower and yard tools, a stack of old aluminum hurricane shutters, piles of boxes, a refrigerator, and, most important, a workbench with cabinets above it. That's where she put together the potions and amulets that were too messy, hazardous, or smelly to work on in the kitchen.

The dragon wandered around the garage, exploring, sniffing. Occasionally he stood on his hind legs to get a better view. His wings remained folded on his back, the broken one at a painful-looking angle. He climbed up a stud of the unfinished wall to the windowsill with ease.

Missy opened the window for him, and he sniffed the air outside.

"You must be hungry," Missy said. "What do you like to eat?"

"Cats."

"They're not on the menu here. What else?"

"Dragons eat a lot of meat, any kind of meat. Preferably fresh. Even better, alive. And mangoes."

"Mangoes?"

"I can't speak for other dragons, but I really like mangoes. And you have a mango tree with fruit—I can smell them." He gestured with his nose at the open window.

"They're not quite ripe yet," Missy said.

"How long am I going to stay here? Long enough for them to ripen?"

"I'm calling a doctor to look at your broken wing. He'll let you know when you can travel safely on your own. But where would you go? Where is home?"

"Florida is my home. At least the Everglades. That's the best place for dragons, though we have to cross over into the other world frequently for safety. But now that *thing* has been hunting us."

"So, what are you going to do?"

"First, I have to find my mother. The last I saw her was in the other world when that thing was chasing me."

It sounded like Ronnie needed much more help than medical care. But Missy didn't know what she could do for him.

Dr. Tobias Hyde was the rare doctor who made house calls. In fact, that was all he made since he no longer was allowed to practice medicine in any hospital, and he could care for patients in an office for only as long as it took for state inspectors to find it and shut it down. Missy never found out what he had done to lose his medical license and spend some time in jail, but it didn't matter now. He was a good general practitioner and surprisingly open minded for a man of science.

"No way. It can't be a dragon," Dr. Hyde said on the phone.

Okay, so maybe he wasn't so open minded.

"You can make the judgement once you see him," Missy said.

He agreed to come to her house that afternoon. She met him at the front door and took him through the house to the garage. His slight, studious appearance belied the fact that he was courageous enough to care for vampires, werewolves, and other monsters.

When Dr. Hyde stepped into the garage, his mouth dropped open at the sight of Ronnie sunning himself on the windowsill.

"Holy Moses, it *is* a dragon."

Ronnie opened his eyes and regarded the doctor. "What is he going to do to me?"

Dr. Hyde's mouth dropped open even further. Missy worried that his jaw had been dislocated.

"It talks?"

"*He* talks. His name is Ronnie. Ronnie, this is Dr. Hyde and he's simply going to help your wing heal."

"I'm not a veterinarian and I certainly don't know much about reptiles, or birds," Dr. Hyde said, approaching Ronnie carefully and peering at his broken wing. "Though I do understand why you couldn't take him to a vet."

"You've treated many patients whose physiology is quite different than normal humans. Who knows, one of these days we might have a lizard-man who needs care."

"How did it break its wing?"

"Why don't you ask *him* how he broke his wing?"

"It was a stupid cat, okay?" Ronnie said. "It's kind of embarrassing. I'd rather not talk about it."

"Cats can be deadly little monsters," Dr. Hyde said. "I don't see any wounds or scratches on you, correct?"

"Yeah."

He gently manipulated the broken wing and unfolded it to reveal that it was actually bigger than Ronnie's body. He ran his hand along the wing's surface, tracing the locations of the bones.

"Does that hurt?"

"Yes, and you can't imagine how much self-control it's taking to stop myself from burning your arm to a crisp."

Dr. Hyde stepped away from the dragon. "My apologies. I don't think we'll need to take you to my house for an x-ray. It appears that the break is in your radius and it feels as if the broken ends of the bone are in close proximity. We'll just tape it up and you'll need to take it easy for three to four weeks."

"I'm going to be stuck here for a month?"

"Well, you can walk places," the doctor said. "I don't know how safe that would be for you."

"Let's see how it goes here," Missy said. "Remember, the mangoes will be ripening soon."

That seemed to cheer Ronnie up. He cooperated while Dr. Hyde wrapped medical tape around his wing and body.

"How do you feel?" the doctor asked.

"Stupid," Ronnie said.

"Let's see if you're able to move about easily enough."

Ronnie climbed down from the windowsill, his claws digging into the wood. He walked around on the garage floor, and then sprinted to the far wall.

"We'll see if I can hunt on foot. I'm used to swooping down

from the sky upon my prey." He turned to Missy. "Can I practice on a cat?"

She shook her head.

"How much do I owe you, doctor?" she asked.

"No charge," he said, "as long as you let me see him again to make sure the bone heals. And to conduct a more extensive examination. This could be my only chance to see a dragon in person. What does he eat?"

"He's an omnivore, but he seems to prefer small animals."

He glanced at Ronnie who was scratching himself with his hind foot.

"He might have mites," Dr. Hyde said. "Give him a bath and keep him in the water for at least thirty minutes. That will kill most of them. Then spread olive oil on his skin to suffocate the rest of them."

"No one is rubbing oil on my skin," Ronnie said, smoke drifting from his nostrils.

"Okay. Next time I see him I'll bring an insecticide spray."

"The olive oil doesn't sound so bad after all," Ronnie said.

"Stay out of trouble, Ronnie," the doctor said as he left.

Ronnie laughed. "Trouble is my middle name. Even though I don't have a last name."

5

LOST VAMPIRE

Agnes Geberich looked at the three other vampires sitting around the table at the emergency meeting of the Squid Tower Homeowners Association Board of Directors. They all looked as worried as she was. One chair was empty. It was where Leonard Schwartz would have been sitting.

"I just got off the phone with our attorney," Agnes said. She had a gruff voice and a hard-to-place European accent. "She can't find where Schwartz is being held."

"And she calls herself a lawyer?" Bill said with plenty of sarcasm.

"She's a very good lawyer, an extremely expensive lawyer. And she's the only decent human lawyer we've found who will discretely work with vampires."

"Can you lay out for us all you know about what happened?" Gloria asked.

"Oleg Kazmirov said that he and Leonard flew into Miami from the Dominican Republic."

"What on earth were they doing in the Dominican Republic?"

"Young women," Bill said. "There's a lot of sex tourism there, and you know how Schwartz is."

Several members groaned in exasperation.

"That's disgusting!" Gloria said.

"As I was saying," Agnes continued, "they were stopped at Customs because Schwartz was carrying vials of blood."

"What's wrong with bringing in-flight snacks with you?" Kim asked.

"You can't bring non-packaged food products across international borders," Bill mansplained.

"It was werewolf blood," Agnes said. "Apparently it's an aphrodisiac for vampires. Particularly those who have trouble raising the flag."

Another group groan of exasperation.

"They both were sent for a secondary screening in separate rooms. Oleg was questioned, his luggage was searched, and he was detained for the rest of the night and most of the next day. When he was released, he found out that Schwartz was still in custody and had been transferred elsewhere. That's when I called our attorney. She made inquiries first with Customs and Border Protection. They said that Schwartz had been uncooperative and verbally abusive—"

"That's our boy, all right!" Bill said.

"And he was in possession of suspected contraband."

"It was just blood," Kim said. "He could have claimed he needed transfusions."

"He was supposed to declare it on his Customs form," Agnes said. "And the implication was that they suspected it was drug related. CBP notified the Miami-Dade Police who then arrested him."

"Oh boy," someone muttered.

"That was two days ago, but there was no record of him being booked into the jail. Finally, our attorney called tonight with news that Schwartz had been taken from Miami-Dade custody by ICE."

"Why ICE?" Kim asked. "What would they want with him? He's a natural-born American citizen."

"No one knows," Agnes said. "It's not common for ICE to take custody of a citizen. And they have no record of him being in their custody. Our attorney thinks he might have been taken by rogue agents."

"What are we going to do?" Gloria asked.

"This is serious, folks," Agnes said. "It's only a matter of time before they discover he's a vampire, if they haven't found out already. Then they're going to come here, and we'll all be in danger of being discovered. And being destroyed."

The room was silent for a while except for a buzzing sound coming from Gloria's hearing aid.

Kim asked, "What about the home-health nurse who's a witch? The one who runs the creative-writing workshop? She can cast a locator spell. At least that's a start."

Everyone nodded in agreement.

MISSY'S PHONE VIBRATED. It was her night off, when she didn't have any patients to visit. She was bingeing on TV episodes and a tub of ice cream. She almost threw her stupid phone across the room, until she noticed it was Agnes' number.

"Hello, what can I do for you, Agnes?"

She listened to a long story from the very upset vampire.

"Okay," Missy said. "I'll be there in twenty minutes."

She collected her magick gear, made sure the cats weren't out on the screened porch, and locked up the house. Before she left, she went to the garage to check on Ronnie. He was sleeping, curled up on folded blankets atop a stack of boxes. He didn't stir, so she let him get his much-needed rest.

MISSY COULD HAVE CAST the spells at her home, but being at Squid Tower made them stronger because Schwartz's energy lingered where he lived. Like some residents would say, it clung to the place like a bad odor. He wasn't exactly the most popular guy.

She stood outside the door to his condo on the third floor. It was morning now and all the vampires should be in bed, so she wouldn't be disturbed. She cleared her mind with some simple meditation techniques, then concentrated on images of Schwartz in her memory: his bald head, bushy eyebrows, big nose, pugnacious expression. And the ear hair, couldn't forget that.

Next, she cast tracer spells, one after another like tiny bursts of air, increasing in frequency as she went. These were like miniature drones made of magick. She aimed them, released them, and let them explore on their own. If they recognized the object of her search, they would "ping" her with their general location. Then she could do a more powerful locator spell that was more accurate and comprehensive—but also more time consuming and power draining.

The tracer spells didn't last long or travel more than a couple hundred miles, so rather than send them out in every direction, she first concentrated them to the south in the Fort Lauderdale-Miami area. A second salvo went more to the southwest, through the far western suburbs of the metro area, and into the Everglades.

Tracer spells usually relied on visual matches, although you could also direct them based on other senses such as smell or hearing. The more powerful locator spell could find things using more sophisticated search criteria, but the tracer spells were the most efficient way to begin a search.

Nearly two hours went by with no response. If Schwartz were imprisoned, it would be much harder to locate him, so she next sent out spells based on her memory of Schwartz's voice and directed the spells to seek that sound. She also directed them to look for visual clues of a jail or prison, such as building complexes with small barred windows surrounded by walls topped with barbed wire.

It was a long shot. And, sure enough, she didn't hear back from a single tracer spell. She was tempted to give up, but she decided to try even harder using her locator spell.

She would assume that Immigration and Customs Enforcement was lying about having no record of Schwartz, or at best had made an error. She went online and found the addresses of ICE detention centers. There were five in Florida. Unfortunately, ICE also sent detainees to privately run facilities. And there was the possibility they could have flown him out of state. She read that there were more than 200 facilities nationwide that held immigrants and refugees.

With the amount of power a locator spell required, checking all those addresses would take months. It was simply not practical. But she had to try at least one.

The closest facility to where Schwartz had been taken into custody at the airport was the Krome Service Processing Center on Tamiami Trail, west of Miami on the edge of the Everglades. She looked it up on her phone's map app, switched to satellite view, and zoomed in so she could form a mental image of the property.

It was time to begin her spell.

When creating her more potent magick, she needed methods that stimulated all five of her senses. Drawing a pentagram with chalk on the tile floor of the hallway channeled the earth-energy she needed, but it also served as a visual trigger that stimulated her own internal energy. The invocation she chanted summoned magick while also engaging her sense of hearing. Incense helped with her meditative state while stimulating her sense of smell. A drop of her blood upon her tongue was for her sense of taste, and her sense of touch came from grasping the power charm she kept in her pocket.

Kneeling within the circle, she went through all the steps of the spell, and by the time she was finishing the invocation the power was surging within her. It was a combination of an adrenaline rush, heightened senses, and religious ecstasy. She felt as if she were leaving her body and floating above it.

And soon her consciousness was floating above the Krome Service Processing Center. She soared over the flat white roofs of the different buildings, among the humming of the air-conditioning condensers. She smelled the lush, green wetlands beyond the double chain-link fences. She moved over the building that contained the largest concentration of human energy.

Her vision didn't penetrate the roof like a spy camera, but instead gave her a more abstract, composite view of the men inside among rows and rows of steel bunk beds in gigantic rooms. But there was no indication of Schwartz among them.

The life force in here radiated boredom and despair, rage and anguish, frustration and fear. A deafening cacophony of voices in Spanish, Creole, Arabic, and languages she didn't recognize rose from the rooms. Desperate to get away, she searched for Schwartz but didn't see, hear, or sense him.

The waves of emotion buffeted her like turbulence shaking an airplane.

The hopelessness was seeping inside her. Dark thoughts of death tried to pull her out of her spell.

She started to panic. But the strangest idea came to her: She could harvest this negative energy. It wasn't dark, evil, supernatural energy—it was only the power of human spirit. As destructive as it could be, it was nevertheless innocent.

Allowing the fear and anger and despair to flood inside her without becoming sickened was difficult. But she found some place deep inside of her where she stored it.

Somehow, she was certain it would come in handy in a battle to come.

After she had sealed off this pocket within her, she pulled herself out of her trance. She reached across the floor and wiped away a small portion of the magick circle. Breaking the circle ended the spell.

Her knees ached from kneeling on the hard tiles of the hallway. Glancing at her watch, she was surprised that hours had gone by while she was entranced by her spell. She was exhausted and needed to go home for some sleep.

More so, she was emotionally drained and battered. There was no way she could perform this spell for every one of the 200 or so facilities where immigrants were detained. He might not even be in any of them.

She could think of only one other thing to do. If she couldn't locate him, maybe she could at least ascertain if he were still alive. Or, more accurately, still undead. Vampires are only immortal if they feed regularly and aren't destroyed through staking, decapitation, or burning. If the authorities discovered

Schwartz was a vampire, they could have summarily executed him. It happened on occasion, probably more frequently than she imagined.

Despite what the haters say, vampires do have souls. And she knew a spell that could tell if a particular individual's soul was still on the earth or had departed for the afterlife. She had never cast this spell before and wasn't exactly sure she could pull it off. She was a little frightened to try it. She had heard that a witch could die if there was a mishap.

It involved contacting a departed soul. And in order to connect with another soul, you put your own at risk.

A perfect metaphor for finding a life partner, she thought.

On her next day off from work she tried it inside the pentagram she drew upon her kitchen floor. The spell was not a telekinetic exercise involving manipulating the physical world with her mind and earth magick. Rather, it was a journey out of her body and away from her mind. Unlike with the locator spell, it was also a journey to another plane of existence.

She burned some frankincense, breathing in the smoke which put her in a mild hallucinogenic state. She immersed herself in chanting a prayer of the native Calusa people she had added to her grimoire, and then chanting it backwards. Drawing from the recesses of her body the pure power that she had inherited from the parents she never knew. Reaching out and dipping the fingers of her consciousness into the powers of the earth. Then, finally, opening her super-stimulated mind beyond its previous limits.

A yawning chasm appeared before her.

She entered the In-Between, the state of existence between life and the afterlife, between the world and Heaven or Hell. Here, she was in danger of slipping into the afterlife, or, worse, being trapped in this state between being and non-existence.

The landscape was an empty, windswept beach that stretched to the horizon with only a glimpse of sea. She had heard, though, that this world could appear to be different each time you visited it. She figured the scenery was illusory and did not truly exist.

She was not alone here. There were lost souls wandering in anguish. She couldn't see them, but they whispered and sobbed in her ear, begging for assistance to reach the afterlife.

Another serious risk was that a soul would try to follow her back to the material world. If it succeeded, it would be trapped on earth as a ghost. Missy would have to endure the guilt for allowing that to happen. Or, she could end up suffering if the spirit didn't release its grasp on her and haunted her forever.

She pressed on anyway.

"Leonard Schwartz, are you here?" her spirit-voice called out, again and again.

There was no answer. Hopefully, that meant he was not here.

She had no right to do it under the laws of God, but the way this spell worked was to make a bargain.

"Who will help me?" her spirit-self called to the lost souls around her. "Who will search for the soul I seek in return for help reaching Heaven?"

More invisible souls swarmed around her like gnats. They were excited, frustrated, frightened.

"Speak out," she commanded.

"Me, I'll do it," a young girl's voice whispered in her ear like a kiss. "My mother is waiting for me in Heaven."

"I will help you make the final step of your journey," Missy's spirit-self said. "As soon as you arrive, you will ask if the soul is there of Leonard Schwartz of Brooklyn, New York, most recently a vampire. Tell me as soon as you find out."

The girl agreed. And Missy gave her a brief, flash-charge of her power. It was just a little bit of energy, not enough to risk Missy slipping out of The In-Between. All these souls needed to complete their journeys was a small bit of power, like a push to help someone up the final step of a staircase. Unfortunately, she didn't have enough power to help more of them. Nor did she have the right.

The girl gasped. And then was gone.

It seemed like mere seconds later when the girl's voice came to Missy:

"They tell me Leonard Schwartz is not here. And he's not in Hell, either. Thanks for your help. Mommy says thank you, too."

Through the process of elimination, Missy was fairly certain now that Schwartz's soul was still in the material world. Schwartz was alive and on earth.

Just as she was pushing her mind into the passage back to the material world, movement caught her eye. Far away, something was rising above the towering dunes along the horizon. A giant, dark figure with the horns of a bull and dozens of eyes in its head. Familiar eyes.

The eyes found her.

Would the creature follow her back home?

Missy woke up on her back on the tile floor of her kitchen. The candles she had burned were melted almost to the ground. She was panting and sweating profusely, relieved to be back in this life. She realized the In-Between must be the world where Ronnie and his mother went to hide, though somehow they managed to travel there physically, not just their spirit-selves as in Missy's case.

She was certain of this. As certain as she was that the multi-eyed monster that she saw there was the same entity that had been chasing Ronnie.

She found Agnes in the property management office on the first floor. Agnes was speaking with fellow board member Kim, who also served as a de facto property manager since it wasn't a good idea to hire a human for that job. They looked up expectantly as Missy appeared in the doorway.

"I'm sorry," she said, "but I haven't gotten any results on my search. The only good news is that he's still alive. My guess is that he's confined in a maximum-security facility with limited access to the outdoors or even windows. I think that's why the tracer spells didn't work."

"Our attorney can't find him," Agnes said. "If you can't either, what are we to do?"

"Hopefully, I can find him with a locator spell," Missy said. "I've already tried one and came up empty. The spell takes a lot of time and power to cast, and if we can't narrow down the number of places to direct it, I would need weeks or months."

"Should we hire a private detective or something?" Kim asked.

"I have a friend who's a reporter with the *Jellyfish Beach Journal*," Missy said. "I'll see if he can help us."

"By the way, you look exhausted, dear," Agnes said. "I would recommend a pint or two of O-positive blood if you weren't human."

"Maybe I'll just take a nap," Missy said.

6

SLIPPERY ICE

Because Missy lived a largely nocturnal lifestyle to accommodate her vampire patients, she didn't get together with Matt Rosen very often. He made it clear that he would prefer to see her much more frequently. She felt a little guilty setting up a breakfast meeting, at the end of her day and the beginning of his, when it was the result of an ulterior motive.

"You need me to be your investigator," he stated in a flat voice as he pushed a piece of French toast around his plate. He was cute, a bit nerdish with his scholarly bearded face, but his dark sunglasses and shaggy brown hair offset the nerd effect.

"I'm just picking your brain," she said.

"If I happened to have heard that an elderly vampire was in custody in an ICE facility, don't you think I would have told you?" He acted peeved. This would pass. "Normally, I would have written a story about it and become famous, but I'm honoring my promise that I would keep your creatures out of the news. And that I would remain toiling in journalistic obscurity."

"And I appreciate your sacrifice." She was starving, but it was hard to enjoy her eggs when Matt was sulking over the fact this wasn't a true breakfast date.

"Sarcasm noted," he said before taking a bite of bacon.

"I did a bunch of spell work looking for him. I'm pretty sure he's alive. And not in the nearest ICE lockup. I checked one of them, a "service processing center," but I couldn't find Schwartz there. I simply can't check every single ICE facility in the state or the country."

"I agree with you. If the attorney can't locate him and ICE swears they don't have him, then Mr. Schwartz is off the books and that's pretty scary. That's like an authoritarian-government kind of situation. But my best guess, assuming this isn't a total dystopian nightmare with secret prisons, is that he's in a private, corporate prison. Private prisons are supposed to share records of their inmates, but they just don't have the account-ability that government prisons face. And prison corporations tend to have lots of lobbyists and make big contributions to politicians."

"So, what do we do?" she asked.

"I don't know. Let me look into it. Maybe I can call in some favors. I'm pretty tight with lots of city and county bureaucrats, but not any Feds. Maybe my sources can give me a lead or two. I'll do my best and let you know what I find out."

"That's all I can ask. I appreciate it," she said. She was begin-ning to enjoy her scrambled eggs at last, before they grew cold.

MATT HADN'T WANTED to admit to Missy that he was in way over his head with his promise. He wasn't much of a crime reporter, because there wasn't much crime in Jellyfish Beach. He'd been to the county jail before to interview prisoners for stories, but the workings of the corrections industry as a whole were totally foreign to him.

So he sat in the empty newsroom of the *Jellyfish Beach Journal*, throwing and catching a rubber ball that he bounced off the wall above the assignment editor's desk with all the corny motivational quotes on it. The main room was empty on a Sunday afternoon, though he heard a televised football game in the room where the sports writers sat, probably watched by an intern who didn't get sent down to Miami to cover the Dolphins game.

Okay, time to stop procrastinating. First, he did some basic research on private prisons. He was astounded by their astronomical growth. While the overall prisoner population grew at a small rate in Florida, the growth rate in private prisons was more than 200 percent. There were a couple of private-prison corporations based in Florida and business was booming, to say the least.

He learned that ICE housed many of its undocumented immigrant detainees in private correctional facilities, to use the correct term. That strengthened his resolve to investigate in this direction, but it widened, rather than narrowed, his search.

So, now what? He couldn't contact every single facility and ask them if they had Schwartz, especially since ICE was claiming they didn't have him. He couldn't use magick like Missy to snoop into them.

It was time to return to the fundamental question: Why was ICE interested in Leonard Schwartz? Were they mistaking him for some other guy by that name who was undocumented? Or a guy by that name who was an activist working on behalf of undocumented people? That last thought was somewhat intriguing.

Or, did ICE know Schwartz was a vampire? How would they have found out? And, most important, what did they intend to do with him?

Matt called his friend and mentor Harold Welk, a semi-retired columnist who used to work for the big dailies in South Florida before easing himself into the slower pace of Jellyfish Beach.

"Make it fast, Matt," Harold said. "I'm stalking a school of redfish."

"Why did you answer the phone when you're out fishing?"

"A bad habit I picked up from this business of ours. What do you need?"

Matt explained the situation with Schwartz as succinctly as he could, leaving out the fact that he was a vampire.

"I feel like I'm at a dead end," he added.

"I have a source, a retired CBP agent," Harold said. "I seem to recall her being involved in a similar situation. I'll send you her contact info. Tell her I told you to call."

Matt thanked him profusely and let him get back to his fly fishing. A text with the source's name and number came through and Matt called.

"Ms. Jabinsky? This is Matt Rosen with the *Jellyfish Beach Journal*. Harold Welk gave me your name. Do you have a moment?"

"Um, okay. I'm at my grandkid's soccer game so I can't talk for long." Her voice sounded too young for a retired person.

"Thanks. This is about a recent incident with ICE taking a

person being questioned by CBP." He went on to describe the story.

"Ah, they're still up to it," she said.

"What do you mean?"

"It happened to me once, ICE stealing a subject I was interrogating. And it wasn't an illegal or a terrorist or a political activist. It was just a stupid clown."

Matt laughed.

"No, really. It was a clown. An evil clown. He was on a charter flight filled with clowns returning home from a clown convention in Germany. And no, they weren't in full makeup and costumes— you're not allowed to fly wearing a costume or disguise."

"Then how did you know he was a clown?" Matt asked.

"Well, first of all, this guy's natural features made him look like a clown. He had a huge pink afro, and a reddish, bulbous nose. But those were just unfortunate accidents of birth. It was his oversized, floppy shoes that were a dead giveaway."

"Why was he pulled aside for inspection? I mean, aside from the shoes."

"The knives and meat cleavers in his checked luggage. And the fact that all his teeth were filed into sharp points."

"Okay," Matt said. "It really was an evil clown. Good call to detain him."

"Then an ICE agent shows up out of nowhere with paperwork to take the clown away."

"But how would he know about the clown?"

"Exactly," she said. "I think someone from our team was on the take. He got paid to inform this 'ICE agent' when he spotted certain characters."

"I couldn't help but hear the sarcasm when you mentioned the ICE agent."

"Yeah. The paperwork the agent gave me was full of errors, and afterwards, when I studied it more, I began to think it was bogus. So I called up a friend of mine at ICE, and you know what? That guy that took the clown wasn't with the agency anymore. He got busted for smuggling and narrowly escaped a murder conviction."

"What's his name?"

"Bill Jaffe, if I recall."

"So he's into collecting evil clowns now?"

"Nah, ex-federal agents who were busted for smuggling aren't usually into hobbies like that. I'm sure someone was paying him to pretend he's still an agent and steal our detainees."

"Why in the world would anyone want to steal an evil clown?" Or a vampire, Matt thought.

"Your guess is as good as mine," she said. "Good luck figuring that out."

Right, Matt thought. I need sheer luck to make any sense of this.

If he made the assumption that an imposter ICE agent took Schwartz as in the case with the evil clown, he could no longer assume Schwartz was in a facility used by ICE. He could be anywhere, even locked up in someone's garage.

And Matt struggled to come up with a hypothesis for *why* he was taken. Why would someone want dangerous freaks?

He bounced the rubber ball against the quote on the wall about perseverance and caught it one-handed. Every time he worked with Missy, he entered the land of freakiness. And once you were in that land, logic went out the window. After he abandoned that pesky logic, it became easier to speculate.

So, assuming the same individual used forged papers to take

both the clown and Schwartz, who paid him to do so? And why?

Still using the freaky non-logic, he thought that the person who paid to have the freaks taken could potentially have more than just the two of them. Matt only recently discovered that vampires and werewolves existed. Who knew what other kinds of supernatural creatures were out there? The person who wanted the evil clown and the vampire might be holding additional creatures.

If that were the case, this person would need a secure place to hold them, not just a garage or mother-in-law apartment. Someplace like a jail or a prison.

But now he was back to square one. Florida was full of correctional facilities, county-run, state-run, Federal-run, and privately operated. Where and how should he check them out?

He threw the ball with too much force and missed it when it bounced back. A crash of coffee mugs came from a cubicle behind him.

He turned on his computer and searched for information about the rogue ICE agent. There wasn't much. Bill Jaffe had worked out of the Miami field office until he was arrested in a town called Eden, Florida. He escaped prosecution for having killed his partner in the smuggling operations by claiming self-defense, but he was sentenced to five years for the smuggling. He disappeared off the map after that.

Then Matt scrolled through recent news stories about prisons in Florida. One caught his eye about a facility south of Miami. He texted the assignment editor requesting permission to work on the story. The editor quickly replied with a yes. He seemed to prefer it when Matt was away from the newsroom as much as possible.

MATT MET MISSY FOR BREAKFAST. Again. It was her preference. Nothing said, "This is never going beyond a platonic relationship," more than invitations to breakfast or brunch. At least he was eager to see her to share his thoughts about the investigation.

He watched her sip her tea at the cafe across the street from the beach. Her eyes looked as if she hadn't been getting enough sleep. He explained what he'd learned about the ex-ICE agent.

"I got myself assigned to work on a story about a private prison south of Miami," Matt said. "It's been under scrutiny by journalists because they're holding migrant kids seized at the border when seeking asylum. I have no idea if they would have Mr. Schwartz, or why. But the rogue ICE agent who took him into custody used to work out of Miami, and ICE dumps a lot of detainees in private prisons. It's worth a look. I don't think it would cause an alarm if I snooped around a bit near that facility, because there are reporters showing up daily there."

"Matt, that would be so awesome if you would do that for us."

"You realize that this is a real long shot, right? First, that he's even there. And even if he were, I don't see how I could find that out for sure."

"I understand," Missy said. "It's safe to assume that whoever is holding him knows by now that he's a vampire. And that's a crisis for us. They could kill him ex-judicially, like the few cops who have encountered vampires have been known to do. And then they could come after all the vampires in Squid Tower. And all over Florida."

"If I find out he's there, maybe there are some legal maneuvers you can use to box the prison company in, because they wouldn't want this to be public knowledge. It would be easier for them to just release him."

"Possibly," she said. "What can I do to help you?"

He was tempted to make a sarcastic remark about giving him moral support, but smiled instead. "I'll let you know."

7

DEMON WANTED

Morgan Dreadrick was trying, for the millionth time it seemed, to summon a demon. He let out a loud, body-wracking sneeze. The expensive incense he burned bothered his allergies.

He wore a tailored sorcerer's robe made from rare mulberry silk, monogrammed with his initials. The robe was jet black with accents of scarlet. It was too hot for Florida weather, so he wore it only when he was in his air-conditioned sorcery room.

These days, any schmuck with a mansion had a theater, a game room, and a bowling alley. But he was the only rich guy with a sorcery room. It was decorated like a dungeon and he had added rare instruments of torture from the Spanish Inquisition he had purchased from the antiquities black market.

The room had a state-of-the-art entertainment system with surround sound and banks of giant-screen televisions. He had figured that adding a multimedia component to his magic should have made his spells easier to cast and more powerful. It didn't seem to have any effect. But watching horror films in the dungeon atmosphere was pretty awesome.

Tonight, however, the televisions remained off. Instead, he pored over a pile of books on a table in the center of room, mostly antique grimoires and volumes on demonology. The table, should anyone ask, was adapted from an original Incan stone sacrificial altar looted from a museum in Peru. The deeply ingrained blood stains made an interesting decorative pattern. He was quite proud of the table.

He had been reciting demon-summoning spells for the past hour and a half. And he was losing patience. He still sought a pact with a demon to get beyond his basic spells and tap into some real power.

Beyond greater power, what he desired most of all was what humans had always wanted: immortality. He had too much money to spend in a dozen lifetimes. But if he could live forever, imagine all the decadent indulgences he could enjoy. And how much more money he could make.

To be honest, he was also afraid of dying just like everyone. But he was a superior human being to everyone else. He was used to breaking all the rules that others had to follow. Mortality was one he believed he should be exempt from.

The problem was, he kept striking out. No demon would work with him.

That's why, when the stench of rotten eggs suddenly filled his nostrils, overpowering the damned incense, he was ecstatic. His long-awaited assistance may have finally arrived. He saw nothing, but sensed a presence in the room in addition to the stench. His heart raced with anticipation.

"Asmodeus?" he asked.

There was no answer.

He sneezed. And wiped his nose on his expensive silk sleeve.

"I invoke Thee," he recited from the grimoire in a deep sorcerer's voice, "the Terrible and invisible God who dwells in the void place of the spirit. Hear me."

Still no answer.

"Oh mighty Asmodeus, I beseech thee," he improvised. "Show yourself. Allow me to converse with thee. C'mon, give me a break here."

"Asmodeus isn't available," said a nasally voice.

A withered old man appeared. He was sitting on the back of an American crocodile, the kind found in South Florida and the Caribbean living in saltwater. The man was small and vaguely reptilian-looking. He wore a colorful tunic and robe and looked like a jockey.

The crocodile was old, too, and was missing some teeth. It looked at Dreadrick and hissed.

"Hello," Dreadrick said, beaming. This was his first demon encounter! Even though this strange guy didn't look like a demon. "I'm Morgan Dreadrick. And you are?"

"Agares."

"I apologize, but are you an A-list demon?"

"I'm one of the original Fallen Angels, spirit of Solomon, and First Duke of East Hell. Is that 'A-list' enough for you?"

"Of course, my apologies. I'm Morgan Dreadrick. You've probably heard of me."

"No," the demon said, waving his hand impatiently. "Why did you summon me?"

"I thought we might make a pact, you and me." Dreadrick couldn't resist the urge to rub his hands together like a stereotypical villain. "You help me smite my enemies and I'll give you a little help in some way. If you're interested, I can set you up with some venture capital."

Agares stared at him, locking Dreadrick's eyes with his black, demonic orbs.

"I can perform an individual task, such as smite one specific person. But you must compel me."

Dreadrick smiled. His grimoires contained spells for compelling acts by the demons you've summoned. But he wanted more. One of his favorite tactics as a negotiator was to make sudden, unexpected demands when his opponents thought a deal was close.

"One other thing," he said. "I want you to grant me immortality."

The demon laughed. "Immortality? That's an awful lot for a mere human to ask for. Being mortal is what defines you as a human."

"I'm greater than the average human. If you don't believe me, look up my net worth."

"Even as a duke of hell, I can't make you immortal," Agares said. "You would need an entity more powerful than I to be granted that."

"You mean the Big Guy? Satan? Lucifer? Or, as I call him, Role Model?"

"Not him. He couldn't be bothered with you. There are ancient gods in hell who are no longer worshipped on earth. Higher than me on the organizational chart. I have one in mind. But he would want you to pay a price, make a sacrifice."

This demon was like putty in his hands, Dreadrick thought.

"Name your price." *And I shall lowball you.*

"Child sacrifice like in the ancient times."

Dreadrick snorted. "Get real."

Agares' eyes narrowed in anger.

Dreadrick's trousers burst into flames. He screamed and rolled on the floor, swatting himself with a priceless Twelfth-

Century manuscript about alchemy until the flames were smothered.

"That was uncalled for," Dreadrick said, smarting with pain. Hopefully the burns weren't too serious. He had a healing spell in one of his books.

The demon shrugged. The crocodile hissed.

Dreadrick got to his feet, noting with pleasure that while his trousers were gone, his sorcerer's robe was untouched. Had the demon deliberately spared the robe, or was there actually some magic in it? He was pleased with himself for spending top dollar on the garment.

"In this day and age, you can't sacrifice children anymore," Dreadrick said.

He did have several children available in one of his private-sector prisons. They were migrants seized at the border with Mexico. He could spare one or two of them, but risked losing his government contract.

"That is the price the god I serve demands."

"Is there anything he would accept instead?"

"A dragon, perhaps."

"You mean, like a gold Chinese dragon statue? I think I have a few of those somewhere."

"No. A living dragon," the demon said.

"Dragons don't exist."

"They do. There is a young one in Florida that my master wishes to destroy. If you present him with this dragon as a sacrifice, maybe he will then grant your request."

Sacrificing the children sounded a lot easier, but his company would take such a terrible hit.

"Okay, if I get you this dragon, I get immortality in return?"

"If my master wishes."

"*If?*" Dreadrick asked.

He was famous for his deal-making skills and this most definitely did not sound like a good deal.

"I'm afraid you need to sweeten your offer," Dreadrick said. "You're losing me, my friend."

"And you have lost me," the demon said, beginning to disappear in a cloud of sulfur-smoke.

"No, please come back!"

The smoke dissipated, revealing the demon had rematerialized.

Dreadrick smiled, thinking he had Agares right where he wanted him.

"What would make our arrangement work better for me," Dreadrick said, "would be your promise to allow me to summon you from time to time to perform acts of evil. I'll produce the dragon for you, at my own time and expense. All you have to do is help me out on what I assure you will be rare occasions. As well as pursue my request for immortality."

Agares stared at him with those dismally black eyes.

Pain burst around Dreadrick's right ear. He tried to touch it only to discover an open wound. His ear was missing. It lay on the floor next to his foot. It was a sign he was losing control of the deal making.

"There will be no negotiating," the demon said. "Deliver me the dragon or die."

"You receive the dragon and I keep my life? That's sounds like a deal in which both sides win."

"I will receive the dragon and then I will decide if you keep your life."

"An eternal life?"

The demon didn't answer.

Dreadrick looked at the reddening burns on his now-naked

legs. He drew the sorcerer's robe closed to conceal them. "Can I ask you a question?"

"I will allow one question."

"Why does the god you report to want the dragon?"

"There have been prophesies that this young dragon will become a savior of its species and lead it to glory," Agares said. "Dragons are my master's great enemy."

"So when you think about it, you and I have the same assignment. How about going into a joint venture together?"

"I want that dragon. You who walk this earth will get it for me. If you do not deliver this dragon to me, preferably alive, I will have you tortured and killed. I command legions of demons who will hunt you down wherever you may hide. Do you understand?"

"Gotcha."

The demon shook his head and laughed cruelly. Dreadrick had to check to make sure his other ear was still attached. At least he had hope, for the first time ever, that immortality was a possibility. However distant.

If he could somehow find a dragon.

8
TASTES LIKE CHICKEN

"This is my latest Johnny Hawk story," Bill said to his fellow members of the creative writing workshop in the Squid Tower community room. "This was inspired by current events, uh, specifically the predicament Schwartz is in."

Missy, who moderated the group once a week, knew that Hawk was Bill's adolescent-boy, wish-fulfillment character. Even old vampires could have adolescent boys hidden inside of them.

Bill cleared his throat and read from the printout of his short story.

"Hawk knew that no prison wall in the world could keep out the mercenary, ex-Navy Seal. Hawk wasn't just armed with his MP7 machine pistol, backed up by a Glock 19 and all the magazines he could carry. Hawk also had dozens of grenades and packs of plastic explosives. No wall was going to keep him out and no guard would survive to stop him from rescuing his best friend from illegal confinement."

"Best friend?" Sol guffawed. "You don't even like Schwartz. You called him a putz to his face just a few weeks ago."

"This is fiction," Bill said. "Do you not understand that fiction is, by definition, made up?"

"Well, if it's all made up, then why don't you write about a vampire named Bill who doesn't lose at poker every single time he plays?"

Bill sighed in exasperation. "I'm not writing about stupid poker games played against vampires who cheat. Do you have no appreciation of the long tradition of action tales?"

"I never understood the purpose of reading stuff that's made up," Sol said. "I like to read autobiographies of famous people. I'm only taking this class to learn how to write my memoirs. I've been around for a hundred and forty years, and that's a lot of memoirs to write."

"Sol, can you please let Bill finish his excerpt? The purpose of this workshop is to give constructive criticism."

Sol grunted and sat back in his chair, arms folded. With his bald head and narrow face, he reminded Missy of Nosferatu in a Boston Red Sox T-shirt.

"Now, where was I?" Bill asked, studying his papers. "Okay . . . Perched in a palm tree, Hawk scanned the scene with his high-powered binoculars. It looked like the guards were changing their shift. It was time to go in."

"Speaking of binoculars," Sol said, "Schwartz borrowed a pair of mine and never returned them."

"Do you mind?" Bill said. "I'm narrating a tale here."

"Why would you need binoculars?" Marjorie asked, one of the dozen or so dedicated regulars of the group. "Isn't your supernaturally enhanced vampire vision good enough?"

"Enhanced vision plus high-powered optics equals freaking awesome vision," Sol replied. "My vision wasn't so great before

I was turned, anyway. You think I wear these," he lifted the pair of reading glasses that were hanging from a lanyard around his neck, "as a fashion statement?"

"Can I please continue reading? Bill asked, irritation in his voice. "I'm getting to the part with explosions and violence."

"Schwartz used the binoculars on his balcony to watch the werewolves from next door doing it on the beach. He was such an old horn-dog!"

"Don't say 'was,'" Gladys said. "I'm hoping he's still alive and will return to us."

"And will return my binoculars to me."

"I've been using his parking spot," Marjorie said. "It's the handicapped spot closest to the elevators. His handicapped permit expired like fifty years ago."

"If Schwartz croaks, what happens to his stuff?" asked Martin, who usually stayed quiet during class. "I've never known any vampires who were killed. I have no idea how inheritance laws work when you're hundreds of years old. Some human cousin forty times removed gets everything? It doesn't seem fair."

"Wouldn't be fair for the state to get it either," Sol said.

"You could leave your assets to the HOA," Marjorie said. "That way the rest of us don't get screwed as badly by the next assessment."

"I have a will. And it states that my assets are going to the AARV to help less fortunate retired vampires," Gladys said. "If I happen to die. Which I don't plan on doing. What's the point of being immortal if you're stupid enough to get killed?"

"Don't you guys want to hear the part with the explosions?" Bill asked. "Missy, aren't you moderating this mob?"

"Sorry," Missy said. "I've been preoccupied lately."

"If we get confirmation Schwartz has been staked or burned

or whatever, we should divvy up his stuff," Sol said. "It's only fair—we're like one big extended family here. I'm sure he gave a spare set of keys to someone."

"I think Agnes should get the final say on something like that," Missy said.

The entire group stared at her.

"You don't live here," Gladys said. "You're not even undead."

"Don't pick on her," Marjorie said.

The group devolved into numerous side conversations on whether or not they had the right to inherit Schwartz's possessions and what would happen to his condo. Then things grew heated when Gladys contested Marjorie's right to commandeer Schwartz's parking spot, even though he had never had the right to use it in the first place.

"'Hawk flattened himself against the outer wall and stuck a block of C4 explosive upon it,'" Bill practically shouted against the din, but it was fruitless.

Missy said, "Don't despair, Bill. Your story might turn out to be less fictional than you think."

THE SIGNS of battle were everywhere when Missy opened her front door. Lamps knocked over, books spilled from the bookcase, sofa cushions in disarray, a rug scrunched up into the corner.

And the most disturbing clue of all: a large clump of gray cat hair on the hardwood floor.

Maybe, just maybe, her two cats had been playing rough and it turned into a fight. But Brenda and Bubba were siblings and got along famously, regularly snuggling together. They hadn't created a big ruckus since growing out of adolescence.

The alternative theory was terrifying, and it involved a young dragon.

"Brenda? Bubba?"

Missy searched her tiny house and couldn't find them anywhere, including their favorite hiding spot under her bed. Her stomach was heavy with dread. She couldn't put it off any longer and opened the door to the garage, a space where the cats weren't allowed to go.

There, at the bottom of the pile of boxes Ronnie used as a sleeping platform, lay a burned skeleton with some charred organs still inside.

Missy screamed.

"What, what?" Ronnie said, his head popping out from behind a stack of hurricane shutters leaning against the wall.

"You killed my cats!"

"I sure as heck didn't. Though they almost killed me."

"Then what is that?" She pointed to the skeleton on the floor.

"Oh, that," he said, toothy mouth relaxing. "That's an iguana. Or, was an iguana. You know, your yard is full of them."

"You killed it?"

"Yes. It tasted just like chicken."

She shuddered. "Isn't that kind of cannibalistic? I mean, you're a reptile, too."

Smoke puffed from his nostrils in anger. "I'm a much more advanced species. Is it cannibalistic for humans to eat a hamburger? You and cows are both mammals."

"Sorry," she said. She continued to look at the blackened skeleton with horror.

"I should have cleaned up," Ronnie said, "but I've never been in a human's house before and I'm not up on the etiquette.

Traditionally, dragons leave the carcasses of their prey just outside the mouth of their lair as a warning."

"Where are my cats?"

"Hopefully far away from me. They're vicious, you know."

"No, I don't. What were you doing with my cats?"

"Trying to escape them. I told you, they tried to kill me."

"They got out into the garage?"

"Not exactly. I went inside to watch some TV and was just taking a little look around the house when they ambushed me."

"I don't recall telling you it was okay to go in the house. How did you open the door?"

"I can't fly right now, but I can easily jump high enough to grab that doorknob."

"Your wing is taped to your body. You shouldn't be jumping up and grabbing doorknobs. And fighting with cats. And hunting iguanas. You're supposed to be taking it easy."

"Iguanas are pretty easy to catch. You should try it. Especially since they're eating your garden."

Iguanas were native to the Caribbean and the tropical regions of the Americas, but not to subtropical Florida. In fact, during winter cold spells, Missy had often witnessed cold-stunned iguanas falling out of trees. Originally released into the wild by pet owners, they spread like a plague of locusts throughout South Florida. They'd eaten all the ornamental plants in front of her house and often pooped in her neighbor's pool.

She recently started a vegetable garden in her backyard. She put a mild protective spell upon it, just in case. If she discovered any tomatoes eaten by iguanas, she would have to come up with a spell with higher firepower.

"Stop trying to change the subject," she said. "I want you to stay away from my cats and be more careful while you're healing. I'll put my tablet out here for you. How silly of me not to think that a dragon would watch TV."

When she went back inside, the two cats were sitting at the entrance to the kitchen, waiting to be fed.

"Where were you guys hiding?"

Of course, they refused to say.

9

FAMOUS MONSTERS

It was total random luck that Morgan Dreadrick came across the photo of the dragon in the Everglades. It had become viral, only for a day, but someone he followed on social media shared the original post along with a joke about poor Photoshopping skills. None of the commentators took the photo seriously. It was all a big joke to them.

But not to Dreadrick. He had an ancient, dragon-demanding god to please. Besides, he was already more credulous than the average person about legendary and supernatural creatures. He was rock-certain that many of them were real. Chupacabra, werewolves, Florida's Skunk Ape (and its cousin, Big Foot), vampires—his conviction was that they all existed in the past or present.

Heck, most people didn't believe demons existed. And he once had doubts, too. But he only needed to feel the burns on his legs and the pain of his expensively reattached ear for proof that his belief in them had been right on the money.

Years ago, he had become a dark sorcerer because he

correctly guessed that it would give him the perfect advantage in the corporate world. He used spells to gain insider information to game the stock market. He used them to spy on his rivals. He was able to sabotage their factory openings and turn their public relations events into farces. He even set a rival company's booth on fire at a trade show in Vegas.

But his power went only so far. He wanted to be able to smite his rival CEOs, raze their corporate headquarters to the ground, and turn to stone any politicians who tried to regulate him. And, of course, he wanted to achieve immortality. To take it to the next level in black magic you needed to tap into the forces of darkness. You needed a little help from a demon.

But, for years, no demon would have him.

He tried to build a personal brand of evil, not just to instill fear in his opponents but also to get some evil cred to help win over a demon. He was famous for his recent TED Talk, "Embrace Your Inner Evil," that was shared all over the internet. His book, *Secrets of the Prince of Darkness*, sold well. He tried to gain notoriety as a heartless boss who regularly fired sole providers of large families right before Christmas. He went on hunting safaris in Africa and posed in photos with the endangered species he had killed, then plastered them all over social media. He made Scrooge and the Grinch look like choir boys.

But nothing worked. Because he was a successful businessman, everyone wanted to be his friend. Because he was rich, everyone loved and worshipped him. Like he was a saint, for Pete's sake.

Before Agares, demons wouldn't give him the time of day. But if he could find the dragon in the photo, then he'd have something even better: an ancient god eating out of his hand.

He immediately set up a meeting with a private investigator he'd used before, Amony Bonnard.

"It's a pretty crappy photo," Bonnard said in his French-Caribbean accent as he peered at Dreadrick's phone. "It does look like a little dragon, but it also looks like it was Photoshopped by a third grader."

"I invited you to my office today to hire you to find this dragon. All I ask is for you to work under the assumption it does exist and give a hundred and ten percent effort in finding it. If it turns out the photo is fake, I want proof of that."

"When I'm not doing security work, my wheelhouse is searching for runaways and cheating husbands," Bonnard said. "I've never looked for animals before. Well, except for a couple of stolen racehorses."

"You tracked down that scumbag who embezzled from my company. He was an animal in my view."

"And, Mr. Dreadrick, I'm an ex-cop and intelligence officer. I'm all about hard evidence. I have to admit I don't believe in dragons. I just don't."

Dreadrick glared at Bonnard. The P.I. was a tall black Haitian who wore a suit that seemed well beyond his income. Bonnard was rumored to have killed hundreds of people when he had worked for various Haitian dictators and oligarchs. Dreadrick's employees would never push back against him the way Bonnard was, but he didn't want any of them involved with this project. He also knew that Bonnard was among the best.

"Does it really matter what you believe?" Dreadrick asked. "Find the creature from the photo. Tell yourself it's a genetically modified iguana that breathes fire if that makes you feel better. I don't care what you believe as long as you find it."

After Bonnard left his office, Dreadrick pondered how he could monetize the dragon if the deal with the ancient god didn't work out. It wouldn't be enough to own the wondrous creature on its own merit. That would be a mere hobby. His style was to use every aspect of his life to generate wealth or else he would be wasting valuable time. If he ever found the secret to immortality, perhaps he could spend more time enjoying life for life's sake. In the meantime, he had money to make.

He was the majority shareholder in a large corporation named after himself, of course, Dreadrick Worldwide. Its main focus was the private prison industry. The key to profitability was to cut costs to the bone. Poorly trained guards plus poor food and even poorer medical care for the inmates. Who cares if they complain or die? They're just prisoners! The biggest costs were the lobbyists who fought for draconian sentences for drug offenses. More heads in beds for more years equaled more money for Dreadrick.

The most promising new opportunity was getting contracts to hold undocumented immigrants, the most powerless constituency in the country. That's what gave Dreadrick the brilliant idea: What about getting paid to imprison other out groups? He had a very expensive lobbyist firm handing out to congressmen pre-written templates for bills that criminalized political dissent. It applied to either side of the political spectrum, so he got funding no matter which party was in power. He couldn't even imagine how many prisons he'd have to build to accommodate all the new prisoners.

Were there groups even more vulnerable to exploit? Yes, there were. Supernatural creatures.

TWO DAYS LATER, Bonnard called.

"I've got good news and bad news," the P.I. said. "The good

news is I had the photo forensically analyzed and there aren't any signs of retouching. So it looks like the photo could be real."

"And the bad news?"

"The guy who took the photo was a python bounty hunter. The buzz on social media says he was found dead, apparently strangled by a python. That means I can't interview him and haven't been able to find out more about him."

"What are your next steps, then?"

"I need to find a solid lead. I hired a local guy to hunt for the dragon, a guy who knows the Everglades like the back of his hand. In case the dragon was already captured, I've been canvassing veterinarians because in the photo it looks like the dragon has a broken wing."

"Okay," Dreadrick said. "Don't let up."

"I won't. But be forewarned, this might take a while."

10

SERIOUS JOURNALISM

T he *Jellyfish Beach Journal* was not exactly nationally known for investigative reporting. If it was known at all outside of Jellyfish Beach, Florida, it was for a story that recently went viral: "Naked Florida Man Eats Own Face in Stolen Police Car." That story had the byline of Matt Rosen. Matt would have preferred to be known for more serious journalism.

That's why he had been staying for almost a week in a fleabag hotel on U.S. 1 in Homestead. It wasn't just as a favor to Missy and her patients at Squid Tower. He was up to his eyeballs now on this story, which he was turning into a multipart investigative series.

The private prison—actually a prison camp with tent barracks—housed more than 3,000 asylum-seeking children detained at the border with Mexico. The national news media had covered this story exhaustively, but since the prison was privately run, the media couldn't get inside for a look around.

Matt planned to be the first journalist to get in. How exactly he had no idea. Preferably in a way that didn't get him killed or arrested.

If he saw any signs of Leonard Schwartz, that would be great. But getting a journalistic scoop was even more appealing.

He'd begged and pleaded by phone and email with every official at Dreadrick Worldwide that he could reach. The private prison company simply had no logical reason to grant his request for a tour or to answer his probing questions about details of the children's confinement. They didn't care what he wrote because their only customer was the U.S. Government which didn't want reporters inside either.

He spent his days baking in the sun atop a stepladder across the road from the prison. The prison consisted of several large tents surrounded by a tall chain-link fence covered with opaque green canvas. This was the only way he could get a glimpse of kids being marched around. It was from this vantage point that he got a glimpse of an additional facility. None of the other reporters hanging around outside the prison camp knew what it was for.

It was just past the second compound where the older teenagers were kept. It was a smaller compound filled with shipping containers that had ventilation ducts on their roofs. This compound had higher fences topped with razor wire.

Who was being held here? he wondered. And why the greater security?

Of course, he couldn't find a scrap of information to answer his question. There was no reference to this part of the prison camp anywhere on the internet or in the archives of any news organizations that he searched. His inquiries to Homeland Security as well as Health and Human Services met a brick wall. He stalked the outskirts of the camp and tried to engage prison workers arriving at or leaving work, but none would speak with him. Satellite images from the internet weren't current enough, showing only an empty lot where the compound now stood.

But they did give him an idea.

"I'm not using one of my own drones, dude," Terrence, a photographer from the *Journal* said over the phone. "If there's any chance of it getting shot down, you have to buy one of your own and I'll operate it."

"Agreed. As long as it's not too expensive," Matt said.

"It's gonna be expensive. No sense in flying a cheap toy with a crappy camera."

Matt agreed. He needed a drone operator skilled in both flying and capturing video footage.

"Do they make any with infrared cameras?" Matt asked.

"Dude, now it's really gonna be expensive. Why do you need infrared?"

"I want to see this compound both at day and at night. We'll do our first flyover at night when they're less likely to shoot it down and arrest us."

"Wait, we could be arrested?"

"If you've never been arrested, you're not a true investigative journalist."

"My job is to take pictures of high school football games and tourists swimming at the beach," Terrence said.

"Then, for once you'll have the chance of winning a Pulitzer."

MATT AND TERRENCE stood outside of Matt's pickup truck with its engine left running, parked on the side of the road near the prison camp. The migrant compounds as well as the mysterious third one had security lights along their fences trained upon the ground both inside and immediately outside the fencing. Terrence held the drone's remote-control box while Matt opened the app on his phone that would play the video footage the drone shot.

"Let's just do one pass, over and then back. I didn't mention that we're near the Air Force base—"

"What? Are you kidding me? It's totally illegal to fly a drone near an airbase."

"That's why we're going to be miles from here before they realize what happened."

After copious amounts of swearing and arguing, Terrence finally lifted the drone from the ground, its four helicopter-like propellers whirring. At less than two feet wide, the drone was smaller than the ones that professional photographers used, but it was still expensive to buy.

"Here we go," Terrence said as the drone rose above them then headed toward the mysterious compound. "Stay on your toes because this is going to be brief."

There was enough moonlight to see the tiny aircraft soar about fifty feet above the ground over the compound. It disappeared from view, but Terrence watched it with the GPS tracker and Matt saw the video appear on his phone screen.

The secret compound they targeted was not illuminated with security floodlights like the ones that held the migrant children. But the thermal infrared video showed the compound clearly. Four shipping containers were arrayed evenly spaced in a neat line parallel to each other. The images were crisp black and white, and the objects were well-defined, almost glowing in the light spilling from the neighboring compound. They appeared to be retrofitted for habitation, with the ventilation ducts on the roofs, electrical lines strung to them from a telephone pole, and doors on their sides but no windows.

The camera picked up no sign of anyone.

Once past the compound, the drone turned around and headed back toward Terence. But on this pass, he lowered the altitude and angled the craft, so the camera pointed toward the sides of the shipping containers. The doors had small windows on them that were barred. They had padlocks as well. The containers clearly looked like jails.

As the drone approached the last container, the door didn't appear to have a padlock on it.

The door opened, just as the drone was passing above it.

Three people exited the door, their body heat lighting up the infrared camera. An adult in a guard uniform escorted two teenaged boys from the container. Ever so briefly, the camera caught the image of a man sitting on the floor inside the container.

The guard looked up and saw the drone. He pressed a button on the radio mic attached to his uniform.

"Oh no, we've got to get out of here," Matt said. "Fast."

Terrence cranked up the speed of the drone. Just as the drone crossed over the road and descended steeply toward them, a beam from a high-powered flashlight hit it.

Matt jumped in the cab and closed his door. He hoped his ancient pickup wouldn't let them down. Terrence stood his ground as the drone landed hard beside him. He picked it up and jumped into the passenger seat, the drone cradled in his lap like a small child.

Matt threw the truck into gear and punched the gas, speeding off down the narrow road away from the compounds.

Flashing strobe lights appeared in his review mirror.

"It's probably a rent-a-cop," Matt said.

"Better hope it's not Air Force security."

"What I'm hoping is that there aren't more of them waiting to cut us off."

So he drove and prayed. And after a couple of miles he blew through a stop sign and pulled onto the main road.

They made it back to the motel in Homestead without incident.

ONE-FINGER SALUTE

Missy could think of millions of things better than men, but she had to admit that Matt was actually superior than her tracer spells. Matt, as opposed to her magick, provided exact GPS coordinates of where Schwartz might be so she could aim her locator spell there.

"You can't really see anything inside the secret compound from ground level," Matt said at their usual café, "so I hired a guy to send a drone overhead."

"You could have been arrested," Missy said.

"We almost were. But we did see some strange goings on there. Watch this."

He handed her his phone which was playing the infrared footage and leaned across the table so she could see the screen.

"Wait . . . okay, right there. See that guard leading those kids from the shipping container? Let me pause it and zoom in. See inside the doorway—that man sitting in there?"

"Do you think—"

"Yes," he said. "In any other situation, I would say those kids were being led to the infirmary or something. But if you imagine a scenario in which Schwartz is being held here, then you could jump to the conclusion that he's being kept in that container and the kids were brought there to feed him with their blood."

"That's a huge jump to that conclusion."

"Look closely at the man. He's bald and wearing shorts with dark dress socks! Who dresses like that besides Schwartz? I guess they never had him change into a prisoner jumpsuit."

"I don't know, I can't tell. The video is awfully grainy, zoomed in like that."

"Well, it's a working hypothesis at least. Now you have a location for focusing your spell. If I'm wrong, there's nothing lost."

"Nothing but a lot of my time and energy," she said.

"You volunteered for this."

"True. And thanks for your help."

"Where do I send my expense report?"

"Don't worry." She smiled. "The homeowners association will pay you back."

"I know. But in the meantime, can we get together some-place other than the same café every time?"

"How about the Pancake Palace?"

He laughed. "I meant meeting for something other than breakfast. Like brunch or—I hope this isn't asking for too much —lunch? Maybe even dinner?"

"If you can accommodate my graveyard-shift schedule, I will certainly think about it."

WHEN SHE GOT HOME, Missy put the GPS coordinates into a map app and then studied the satellite view of the nondescript facility. She zoomed in and it did look a little bit like a prison. She then zoomed out to get a better feel where exactly it was located in relation to her. "Get directions" told her it was seventy-eight miles away.

This was the most specific targeting she'd ever had for a locator spell. So she got to work. She drew a conjuring circle with chalk on her kitchen floor, lit candles at the points of an imagined pentagram within the circle, the peak of the pentagram facing south toward the internment facility. She lit some frankincense, then tried to relax and clear her mind. She chanted the Latin words, and went through the other rituals to engage her five senses and connect with her inner powers.

She held the image in her mind from the satellite photo, intensified her concentration, and began summoning the necessary power. Some of it came from within, from the tiny reservoir that every person has. Some of it came from the earth, activated by the mechanics of the spell. And a majority came from the supernatural forces within her. Those she had been born with and lived most of her life not knowing she possessed, until she began the long process of training in magick and learning how to utilize them.

Suddenly she felt the power rush into her, and she felt as if she were in the sky floating above the prison, looking down upon the tops of four shipping containers arranged in a row within a fenced area. She pictured Schwartz's face from her memory. She willed her astral vision to penetrate the metal and see inside the boxes. Two of the containers were occupied by creatures of some sort. She began zeroing in on the first one.

And hit a wall of blankness.

Her vision had already penetrated the roof. Why would it suddenly go dead?

Then she realized what was wrong: A spell of some sort was blocking her. This hadn't happened to her before. Some sort of witch, wizard, or sorcerer was guarding the containers. If she were more experienced, she might be able to identify the spell and disable it, but she didn't know how. She could tell, however, that it was a fairly simple spell. Strong enough to block her, but not sophisticated enough to attack her.

She could also tell that it was black magic, deriving its power not from within the conjuror or from the earth, but from an evil supernatural source. She'd never encountered that before, but she knew it was true from the sick feeling in her gut and the goosebumps running up her arms.

Then, without even trying to summon it, an image formed in her mind. A man with dark hair, a thin nose, and a weak chin. He was wearing a garish black silk robe and a hat with symbols of the arcane embroidered on it. He looked like he was dressed as a wizard for Halloween.

He gave a spiteful smirk and a one-finger salute, then the image disappeared. He had clearly wanted her to know that he was blocking her spell and had gotten the best of her, kind of a witch's version of trash-talking an opponent. It was a typical male dominance display.

He was just a dweeb in her eyes. But it did bother her to know that another witch was an antagonist. Saving Schwartz would be much more complicated—and dangerous—than she had anticipated. She couldn't be positive Schwartz was in one of the shipping containers, but she had a gut feeling now that he was.

It didn't look promising for Schwartz. Maybe the vampires

squabbling over who should get his possessions weren't off the mark after all.

Dreadrick had never had a magical intrusion before. He had placed a type of spell colloquially known as a "burglar alarm" around and above the compound that housed his special-interest prisoners. He hadn't really believed a witch or wizard would attempt to pry into his affairs, but he cast the spell just in case. When it alerted him, he was surprised. At first, he hadn't even realized what the alert was.

After he slipped into visualizing mode, he sensed the foreign spell trying to worm its way into the compound. He immediately put up a protection barrier around the property and felt it deflect the foreign spell. Then he attempted to trace the source of the spell.

A witch. Somewhere in South Florida. It was a woman.

He laughed to himself. There couldn't possibly be a woman witch as powerful as he. Or as brave and ruthless. He glimpsed a faint image of her: pretty, approaching middle age. No one special. Just a chick being nosy and trying to spy on him. Hoping to see if it was true that he was gathering the world's only collection of supernatural creatures that, if made public, would shatter the narrow-minded beliefs of skeptics everywhere.

He gave the other witch the finger to show her how little he respected her. That made him feel good.

It was only later that he wondered why she was trying to snoop on his rumored collection. Maybe she was hoping to rescue one of his prisoners.

No, that was unlikely. Why would a witch want to help a

vampire? But he would have to remain alert just in case. He texted Bullock, the supervisor who was subordinate to the warden yet was the only staffer he trusted to run the Special Collection Unit. He told him to maintain the highest level of readiness.

12

DON'T BITE

No one ever called Leonard Schwartz by his first name. They just called him Schwartz, usually with a tone of exasperation. Even Schwartz called himself Schwartz, as in, "Schwartz, it's time for a nap," or, "Schwartz, you handsome devil." Used with tones of friendship or anger, the name imparted power like a force of nature.

That's why he was seriously offended when the guards called him Schwartz-ula. It was their lame attempt at humor. Get it—Schwartz is a vampire like Dracula? What were these guys, eight years old?

"Hey, Schwartz-ula, I got you some Mexican food for dinner," the big, redneck guard with the crewcut said to him after he unlocked the shipping container door and scanned the inside to make sure Schwartz wasn't going to ambush him.

The guard had two Hispanic kids with him. They were barely into their early teens and were clearly scared to death.

"I don't think I can watch this," the guard said. "So I'll leave 'em here and you can drink as much blood as you want. They don't know what you are, so they won't put up a big fight. At first."

He laughed and slammed the door. The retractable cable that ran from the wall to a plastic collar around Schwartz's neck loosened. The *snap* of a padlock came from outside.

The two boys—they looked like brothers—cowered by the door, watching Schwartz warily. Schwartz had been locked in this tin can with no windows or idea of the time of day, so he didn't even know how long he'd been here. The hunger pains were a clue that it was a long time.

Schwartz never claimed to be a paragon of goodness. He was the first to admit he could be a selfish jerk at times, which was only natural for a guy who never married. He was too quick to escalate disagreements into arguments. "Ornery" was a word frequently used to describe him. And there was that weakness for pretty women who were barely above the age of consent.

But he would never feed upon minors, no matter how hungry he was.

"Have a seat," he said to the kids, gesturing at the floor since there was no furniture in this jail cell. He had been sleeping on the floor atop a smelly sleeping bag.

The kids didn't seem to understand English. And he didn't know Spanish. In the days before he was turned, Brooklyn had very few Latino residents. You could hear lots of Italian, German, and Yiddish spoken on street corners back then but not much Spanish. After he was turned, Puerto Ricans began moving into his neighborhood.

But as he would say to his fellow vampires, it was too hard to learn new languages when you're eternally in your seventies and new languages replaced existing ones as the decades went by. And, besides, why did he need to be able to speak to more people? The only new people he wanted to meet were prey. Even on his fateful vacation in the Dominican Republic, he was able to get what he wanted with English.

So, Schwartz and the two Latino brothers sat on the floor and stared at each other until Schwartz made an effort. He pointed to himself.

"New York," he said. Then he pointed to the brothers and raised his eyebrows.

"Tegucigalpa," the older-looking one said. "Honduras."

"Ah." Schwartz pointed to himself. "My name is Schwartz."

The older brother said, *"Me llamo Felipe. Mi hermano se llama Raul."*

"Nice to meet you."

Schwartz handed them each a bottle of room-temperature water and they drank eagerly. He lay down on the sleeping bag that lacked a pillow and tried to sleep, the overhead fluorescent lighting making it difficult. At least his jail had air conditioning.

A few hours later, the padlock rattled and the security cable that served as Schwartz's leash tightened, limiting him to within six feet of the wall next to the sleeping bag. One time he almost broke his neck when the cable was retracted as he stood near the door. That taught him to get near the wall whenever he heard a guard unlocking the padlock.

The same guard entered the shipping container. The boys stood up quickly, standing close together. The guard roughly grabbed each boy by the chin and examined their necks.

"No bites." He looked at Schwartz suspiciously. "Aren't you hungry? Or are you protesting or something?"

"I'm still waiting to speak to my lawyer."

The guard guffawed. "Lawyer? We never let any lawyers in this place."

"Why won't anyone tell me what I'm accused of?"

"Accused of being a vampire, maybe?" The guard laughed again. "We're a private prison. We just hold people ICE tells us to hold. And I'm just a guard."

He yanked the boys' arms and took them from the cell. Schwartz's stomach rumbled and he worried that he wouldn't be able to resist feeding on the young prisoners much longer.

NOT LONG AFTERWARDS, the padlock rattled again, and Schwartz scooted closer to the wall before his leash tightened.

"Wait outside," a man said before entering.

He was probably in his forties and gave off the air of a rich jerk before he even said anything to Schwartz. He styled his jet-black hair in an expensive haircut that was meant to look a little ruffled and carefree. He wore a gray hoodie over an obviously expensive blue dress shirt, along with charcoal-gray slacks and Italian loafers. The guy wasn't especially tall, but appeared fit in a personal-trainer-created way. Even his finger-nails looked as if money had been spent on them.

"Can I help you?" Schwartz asked sarcastically.

"Yes, you can. I brought you here for a reason."

"Oh, *you* brought me here? As your prisoner?"

"You would have gone to a really rough jail and then, when ICE found out that you're a vampire, you would have ended up with a stake in your heart. I have a mole inside CBP that I pay very handsomely to alert me whenever they come upon a supernatural freak at a port of entry. And I have an ex-ICE agent who springs them from jail. You're lucky that I arranged for him to bring you here."

"Maybe it's the leash that dampens my lucky feelings."

"Do you know who I am?"

"You're my jailer."

"I am Morgan Dreadrick."

"I'm supposed to know that name?"

"My name is always in the news. My face is always on TV. I own prisons all over this country and interests overseas. I buy and sell politicians. I do TED Talks. I even have my own reality show."

"Look, I'm retired. I don't follow the business news so much anymore. Besides, when you've been around as long as I have, it's a waste of time to keep up with whatever humans are famous at any given time before they fade away. It all becomes a blur."

"And that's why you're here. Let me get right to the point," Dreadrick said, crouching down so he was eye level with Schwartz. "I'll set you free and pay you forty grand if you make me a vampire."

"Are you crazy?"

"Fifty grand."

"Why would you want to become a vampire?"

"To become immortal, why else? I'm trying to work out a deal with an ancient god to grant me immortality, but it's still up in the air. You might be my only way."

"You understand that you have to die to become a vampire?" Schwartz asked.

"I'll leave the technical details to you."

"I'm not interested."

"Sixty grand. Now don't be greedy."

"Don't be a cheapskate. That measly amount is nothing to a vampire. I'll have taxes and HOA fees to pay for centuries. But this has nothing to do with money. It's a great responsibility to create a vampire. I'd have to nurse you through the process, teach you millions of things, and then have you around bugging me for the rest of eternity."

"I have no interest in keeping you around."

"You say that now, but you don't understand. You'll be as helpless as a baby. You'll need your maker. And even once you're on your own two feet, you'll have an unbreakable bond with me. Forever. Just like family."

"I turned my back on my family years ago."

"It's different once you're supernatural. Believe me. I'm the least-social vampire around and I still stay in touch with my maker and with my child—the one vampire I made."

"Seventy grand. And I won't go any higher."

"Look, I'm just not into being your maker, understand?"

"Do you know what happened to the last vampire who turned down my offer? I kept him prisoner for years while a researcher performed barbaric medical experiments on him to search for the cause of his immortality. It didn't work. So then I staked him to death. Do you want that to happen to you?"

"It sounds better to me than being your maker. You're too much of a jerk as a human. You'd be even worse as a vampire."

"A hundred grand and that's my last offer."

"Forget it buddy. I'm going to sue you for a thousand times that."

"First of all, I have an army of lawyers. Second, you're never going to speak to anyone outside of these walls again."

"We'll see," Schwartz said, turning away.

Dreadrick stood. "I'm not done with you, vampire. If you knew anything about me, you'd know that I always win."

"Pomposity won't make me like you any better."

"We'll see how you feel once you're starving to death. I'm not sending any more child prisoners for you to snack on."

"I didn't feed on them. But it's nice of you to think of my sustenance," Schwartz said, turning to face Dreadrick again and look at him in the eyes. "I prefer to prey upon adults, not children."

Schwartz's eyes locked with Dreadrick's as he began to mesmerize him.

"Come closer so I can gag at the smell of your overpriced cologne," Schwartz commanded.

Dreadrick bent down again and moved closer to him.

"A little closer. Good. You'll feel a little pinch, and then you'll forget everything that happened after the moment I told you I won't be your maker."

Schwartz gripped Dreadrick by the head and the shoulder before sinking his fangs into the rich man's neck. He drank deeply, feeling his hunger and weakness fade almost immediately. He consumed more blood than he normally would have, not knowing when his next feeding would come or if this would be his last. Plus, he wanted the jerk to feel crappy for a while.

"Go now and forget," Schwartz said.

Dreadrick rose, wobbled a bit, then walked out of the shipping container with a confused look on his face.

"Total schmuck," Schwartz said out loud. "Thinks he can buy everything, even immortality."

13

WHO LEFT THE GATEWAY OPEN?

Missy was driving home at dawn, finishing a night of patient visits of the retired werewolves in Seaweed Manor. She sat at a stoplight near the turnoff to her street and watched the rose-colored light seeping above the palm trees and slash pines. The sky was mostly clear, except for a dark raincloud moving behind the trees.

However, it was moving a little too quickly. It wasn't a cloud. It was a shadow like the one she had seen in the Everglades when she rescued Ronnie. She realized it must be headed for her house.

The light was still red. She hit the gas and sped through the intersection. Half a mile later, she turned into her street, her tires squealing. She always drove slowly here because of kids and dog-walkers, but she was too far away to cast a protection spell for Ronnie. So she didn't slow down, using a spell to heighten her senses in case she had to avoid hitting someone.

Thunder boomed overhead.

By the time she reached her house, the shadow had already extended into a fissure running across the sky from east to west. A jet-black funnel cloud descended from the fissure, like the proboscis of a mosquito, aiming at her house just around the bend.

No tornado warning went off on the radio or her phone. She wondered if anyone else noticed this, or just her.

She pulled into her driveway just as the funnel cloud, now an almost-solid, spinning shaft of darkness, drilled down upon her roof. She leaped out of her car and sprinted for the front door, fumbled her keys, jammed the right key into the keyhole, and burst inside.

The house was vibrating. Not shaking like an earthquake, but quivering in a tight frequency. She feared it would lift off of its foundation. Now that she was inside, she began casting her protection spell, assuming the cats were hiding under her bed and Ronnie was in the garage. She assembled the spell around the entire house.

Something was wrong. The spell wouldn't reach completion. The bubble wasn't sealing itself off. Had the dark power penetrated too far?

"Ronnie!" she yelled. "Ronnie get in here quick!"

As she ran to open the door to the garage, there was a thump against the door, the handle rattled, and Ronnie popped inside.

"Come into the bedroom," she said.

"Where have you been?" he asked in frustration. "I tried to contact you. I could feel it trying to break into our world."

"You contacted me?"

"Yes, telepathically. I thought you would answer."

There was no time to discuss it. Once they were in the bedroom, she drew the existing, though incomplete, barrier bubble inwards. Now it enclosed only the bedroom. She felt it seal properly, and she filled it with more power, strengthening it.

Just then, the house went dark and the vibrating stopped. A tremendous roar echoed in the hallway. Picture frames clattered; glass shattered. She prayed that her house would not be destroyed.

The barrier was hit hard. And again, by increasingly stronger blows. The room shook. She almost fell over. But the bubble did not burst.

Dozens of eyes glowed in the dark around her. Now, after having visited the In-Between, she had more of a conception of what the entity looked like, or at least how it projected itself in material appearance. She used that image to send bolts of force at it. This was difficult, because she had to use much of her power and concentration to maintain the protection spell. But though her bolts may be fairly harmless, they would hopefully distract and weaken the entity.

The darkness faded slightly, and she could make out the details of the room again in the sunlight that made it through the windows. She kept up her assault with the bolts of force.

Then Ronnie screamed. He slid across the hardwood floor as if pulled by a magnet and slammed into the closed bedroom door. He pressed against the bottom of the door, as if the entity were trying to suck him through the crack below the door. Ronnie hissed with pain.

How was the entity doing this? It didn't physically breach the protection spell, but obviously some of its powers did. How?

Missy grabbed Ronnie, careful of his broken wing, pulling him away from the door. The suction force was incredible. As soon as she freed him, he was yanked from her arms and violently slammed against the door again.

She realized the entity wanted to capture Ronnie, but was just as happy to kill him instead.

Missy wasn't powerful enough on her own to defeat this enemy. All she could do is refocus all her energies on strengthening the bubble and hope that it held.

And pray for a miracle.

A miracle came. The pressure pushing against the bubble ceased. The sunlight coming into the room returned to full strength. She felt an absence of tension. The house was silent, and the birds chirped outside. The entity was gone.

"My God," Missy said, breathing with relief. "We are so lucky. I don't know why it retreated."

"Because my mother heard my cries and intervened. She revealed herself in order to lure the entity away from me. It's going after her now."

THE CATS WERE OKAY, just a little traumatized and impossible to remove from under the bed. The ceiling was intact. Inside, pictures had fallen from the wall or became crooked, pieces of furniture had shifted, and various items had fallen from shelves. Aside from that, all was in good shape at Chez Missy.

Ronnie, however, was a wreck.

"All this time I was waiting for Mother to find me. Now she is the one who needs rescuing."

"Where is she?"

"I don't know," he said. "I last saw her in the In-Between before the entity came after us. I escaped back to this world and I assumed she was hiding somewhere. But now it can find her."

"How did she hear your cries?"

"Didn't you know that dragons are telepathic?"

"Um, no." She also hadn't known they could talk.

"I thought you were telepathic, too. That's why I was trying to warn you that the entity was coming."

"No, I'm not."

"I sense that you are, actually," he said. "You probably only need to awaken the ability."

It was increasingly the case that Missy discovered supernatural powers that had been dormant her whole life. Aside from the weak telekinetic ability to move objects with her mind that she'd had since childhood, she had never realized she had the means to draw power from the earth until fairly recently. She now used this power to create magick that had once been beyond her dreams. So it wouldn't surprise her to learn she also possessed the power of telepathy.

"Maybe you're right," she said, "but there's no time to work on that right now if your mother is in trouble."

"I'm afraid that the barrier between worlds has been weakened and the dark entity is getting ready to return to this world. It's still fairly weak, but growing stronger. It shouldn't have been able to break through outside of the Everglades."

"It didn't seem so weak to me," Missy said, though she knew it might be true. Relatively new at this spell-casting game, her powers weren't particularly strong yet. If they couldn't stop the entity on their own now, she couldn't imagine how futile they would be if the entity became greater in power.

"The last time this entity, and others, passed freely into the world, there were terrible wars and diseases on earth."

"You mean the early Twentieth Century, like World War I?"

"No, the early Fourteenth Century. Plagues and all that."

"Did the entity enter the world through Florida back then?"

"I don't know. Probably, even though it was causing havoc in Europe."

"Why would it still use Florida now? You'd think Washington, D.C., would be more appropriate for causing havoc in this country."

"I already told you: This is where the gateway has been, for thousands of years at least," Ronnie said. "Dragons discovered it when humans were beginning to kill us off. Giving us an escape route kept our species alive.

"Then we found out that others were using the gateway as well. This dark entity noticed us, then. It stalked us in the In-Between and followed us to other worlds. It demanded that we offer sacrifices of our young or it would kill our entire species. That's when we fought back. Since then, for eons, dragons guarded the gateway and had their babies in the Everglades, raising them there until they're strong enough to travel to other worlds where they might need to survive an attack by the entity."

"How do you keep the entity from coming through?"

"With magick that only we dragons know. But it doesn't always work."

"Well, we humans owe you guys a lot," Missy said. "I thank you on behalf of all of us."

"I hope you realize that we dragons aren't doing this to protect humans. Y'all have tried to wipe us out throughout history. We're doing this to save the children of the world. The children of all species."

"You need to show me how to use this gateway so we can find your mother," Missy said.

She went outside to check on the exterior of the house. Broken tree limbs littered the yard as if there had been a powerful windstorm, but the house itself looked okay. The standing-seam metal roof was apparently intact.

As she stood in the yard, sirens approached. About a block away, where her street made a sharp turn, a group of neighbors gathered, the flashing police lights highlighting their faces in the early-morning light. They appeared to be looking up at something in the sky.

Uh-oh, she thought.

She walked over, nodding hello to the few neighbors she recognized. She followed their gazes and discovered what they were staring at.

An ice-cream truck was perched twenty feet in the air in the branches of a giant banyan tree. The driver was peering from his open window, clutching the door with terror. The vehicle was small, a converted van, white with pictures of ice cream cones and popsicles pasted to its sides. She often saw it creeping along the street, a loudspeaker playing the same inane nursery tunes over and over and luring neighborhood kids to run after it.

"Isn't it early for an ice-cream truck?" Missy asked no one in particular. "Who wants to hear that music first thing in the morning?"

"How in God's name did it end up there?" a mother asked, holding the hand of her toddler daughter who stared up at the truck longingly.

"Tornado," said a retired neighbor, the guy who was in this front lawn every single time she drove by, crouched by the flowerbeds doing who-knows-what. "Never got a warning but you should have seen the sky. Dark as night even though the sun was up. I saw the funnel cloud over there."

He pointed at Missy's house. She looked away.

"Well, at least we won't have to listen to 'Pop Goes the

Weasel' a hundred and forty times in a row," the mother said. "That is, until he gets the truck repaired."

Missy wanted to laugh, but she had a heavy feeling in her chest. She had assumed the dark entity's powers were directed only at her and Ronnie, but now she saw it could attack innocent bystanders.

And perhaps kill them.

14

HERE THERE BE DRAGONS

Bonnard knew he wouldn't get far asking the Everglades National Park rangers and staff for help. They were too scientific to accept the existence of dragons, and even if they believed personally, they'd probably never admit it. Instead, he looked for private tour guides. Everyone he spoke to said that Billy Turner knew the swamps better than anyone alive. It wasn't difficult for Bonnard to look him up.

"Yes, I believe it is a dragon," Billy Turner said to Bonnard at the boat ramp. "I've seen a couple in my time."

Bonnard smirked. "Yeah, right."

"I don't mind if you doubt me," the old Miccosukee said from the deck of his airboat that he used for Everglades tours. His wide face was in shadow beneath his sweat-stained cowboy hat. "It's best that no one believes in them."

"I'm not saying I don't believe you. I just need to be convinced a little. Do they all look like the one in the picture I showed you?"

"Yes, though that one was kind of small. The bigger ones stay hidden during the day. They burrow into the mud like gators and get their energy from the heat."

"Yes, of course. Cold-blooded reptiles."

"They hunt at night and cook their prey with their fire. Night is the only time you will see them flying. They don't stay long in the Everglades because of humans. They go to a land that is beyond this earth. Where it is, I don't know. But they always come back, especially in the summer when humans are scarce.

"When I was a kid," he continued, "my grandparents told stories of when the first people lived in Florida, long before the white men came. Dragons were plentiful in the Everglades then. When they fought or did courtship rituals, their flames would burn the sawgrass for miles around and drive the deer and other game right into the hunters' laps. I wish the dragons would come more often. We need something to eat the damn pythons."

"How should I look for this dragon?" Bonnard asked. "The geo-tag on the photo says it was near the Pa-hay-okee Overlook. I drove past there on the main road, but I don't know the Everglades."

"*Why* do you look for it?"

"A rich, powerful man is paying me to do it. And I will pay you to help me."

"Rich, powerful men have almost destroyed the Everglades. I would never capture such a rare, magnificent creature for a man like that. I could never take your money."

"You don't have to. I just need to know if it's still here. I worry that someone has already captured him. If you take a picture that proves he's still here I'll pay you a thousand bucks."

"Doing that will help someone else capture it. I can't allow that—there are so few dragons left."

"You're turning down easy money."

"I get a percentage of profits from our casinos. You can't get money that's easier than that. Why sell out my nation and the land we share with such creatures?"

To hell with this guy, Bonnard thought, turning away toward the parking area.

"By the way, if you leave the National Park and go onto our reservation, that's trespassing," Billy said. "And we have our own cops. Just sayin'."

"BANYAN TREE ANIMAL HOSPITAL," an older woman with a nasally New York accent answered the phone.

"Yeah, hi," Bonnard said, struggling with how he was going to say this. "Have you guys ever cared for a dragon?"

"Dragon? You mean a Komodo dragon? We don't handle exotic reptiles. Try the Gulf Stream Vet Clinic."

He sighed after she hung up. This was like looking for a needle in a haystack. He'd been working on this for two days. Searching the internet for dragon veterinarians or veterinarians who mentioned dragons on their websites was a dead end. Obviously, no one cares for dragons which, as far as Bonnard was concerned, shouldn't even exist. The only place that would care for a dragon would be the one random office that this one random dragon was taken to. He'd have to contact every single veterinarian in Florida.

He popped a couple more pieces of nicotine gum in his mouth. Then he dialed again.

"Gulf Stream Vet Clinic," a man answered.

"Have you guys ever cared for a dragon?"

The guy laughed. "Is this April Fool's Day?"

"I'm serious. A dragon. A reptile."

"A Komodo dragon?"

"No."

"Bearded dragon?"

"No," Bonnard tried not to lose patience. "A *real* dragon. Fire-breathing, gold-hoarding. The ones in books and movies with wizards and elves and crap like that."

"Sir, I can refer you to a mental health hotline."

"Don't mess with me. I just want to know if anyone has ever brought a dragon—let's say an exotic lizard that looks like a dragon—to your office. Or if you've heard of another vet seeing one."

"We get all sorts of rare-reptile pets but never anything like a dragon. Aren't they as big as a house?"

"Not this one. And it's not a pet. It would have been rescued from the wild with an injury."

"Maybe you should try a wild-animal rescue center. They have vets."

Bonnard thanked him and hung up. Calling the wild animal rescue centers proved fruitless, as well. Even though he prided himself for having a hard heart, he ended up donating to three of the centers after they mentioned cute, orphaned raccoon babies.

Then he got what he thought was the brilliant idea to contact animal trappers, the folks who took squirrels out of your attic or iguanas from your yard. He even called a couple of alligator trappers.

But no dice. Maybe the dragon was still in the Everglades. He needed to find a hunter like the one who found the dragon before he was strangled by a snake. He called the Florida Fish and Wildlife Conservation Commission which had a program to encourage Burmese python hunting and removal. They offered a prize drawing for people who could prove they bagged a snake, but they couldn't refer him to any hunters. They did tell him that the South Florida Water Management District paid snake bounty hunters directly.

He lied to them, said he was a journalist writing a story about python hunters for a community newspaper whose name he made up. Could they please refer him to some of their most prolific snake catchers? Their public relations flack was happy to oblige and provided five names.

Bonnard called each bounty hunter, planning to repeat his lie about doing an article. He would ask some general questions about their background and why they were bounty hunters, trying to assess how corruptible they were.

The first man wouldn't take his calls. The next was a woman who was skeptical and gave a non-committal yes. The next three men seemed excited about getting their names in the news media. Of the three, two were true believers in the cause of saving the wildlife of the Everglades.

The last man had a different motivation. He wanted revenge. It turned out he was the brother of the hunter who had been strangled by a python while taking photos of a strange dragon-like creature. This man wanted to kill the snake that killed his brother and, heck yes, to kill that damn weird lizard that distracted his doomed sibling.

This man, Bugg Spencer, was fueled by anger and hatred. Bonnard had found the perfect man for the job.

15

FALSE GOD

The next day, Missy went to see Luisa. Luisa's Mystical Mart and Botánica was in a strip center between a beauty supply wholesaler and a taco shop. It was the store where Missy bought many of the supplies for her spell casting and occasionally helped with shelf stocking to earn some extra cash.

Luisa was an expert in Santeria, and knew a lot about Voodoo, obeah, Wicca, and other mystical pursuits. Missy considered Luisa a friend and spiritual advisor. In fact, Luisa was the one who recognized Missy had unusually strong innate powers and encouraged her to take her dabbling in magick to the next level.

But Luisa was stumped when Missy told her about the dweeb in the wizard costume and the dark entity that had been attacking her. That's why she invited ex-Father Marco Rivera-Hernandez. He had been one of the Catholic Church's most prominent demonologists and exorcists in the United States until an exorcism went wrong, and he became possessed himself. The demon, which he carried around to this day, was prone to say politically incorrect things that soon got Father Marco defrocked and excommunicated from the church. Luisa referred him to her customers as a consultant on problems related to spirits and the supernatural.

Missy felt indebted to the priest for his continued encouragement for her to develop her powers. But the dude kind of freaked her out. His demon tended to interrupt conversations and make ex-Father Marco sound like he had Tourette Syndrome.

"Based on what Missy described, it sounds like the man in the wizard costume might be practicing black magic," ex-Father Marco said.

"How is black magic different from my magick? What exactly makes it 'black'?" Missy asked.

"Unlike you, who derive power for your magick from the earth and from your own natural gifts, black magic practitioners depend upon dark, supernatural forces. Demons and evil spirits, in other words. They appease these forces through sacrifices—whether it's as simple as blood on a needle or slaughtering an innocent creature. This magic can be very powerful, but, obviously, comes at a great cost."

"Can black magic help you succeed in business?"

"It can help you in almost everything," ex-Father Marco said. "Except redemption. It affects the material world and the course of events. But black magic uses malevolent power to perform malice, often with unanticipated results. You can cast a love spell with either earth magick or black magic. The black magic spell might work quite well until you realize it's a demented, unhealthy love obsession you created, one that damages both the lover and the loved."

"What about this dark entity that Missy describes?" Luisa asked.

"It's either a super-powerful demon, or perhaps even a god."

"A *god?*" Missy and Luisa both said at the same time.

"Why, yes. We good Christians have our one Heavenly Father, but there have been many, many polytheistic religions throughout history."

"Yeah," Missy said. "But a lot of those religions from the past went away."

"But their gods didn't go away," ex-Father Marco said. "Whether or not you believe in them doesn't matter. Thousands of years of intense faith from their followers gave them their powers which don't simply go away."

"How do you defeat a god?" Missy asked.

"You can't really. You can only distract them or, if you're lucky, make them go back to sleep or back to Hell."

"If this entity is a god, then which one?" Luisa asked.

"Based on Missy's descriptions of bull horns and its demands for the dragons' children, I would guess Moloch. A god of the ancient Phoenicians and Canaanites. One of the false gods that our God commanded the people of Israel not to worship. Moloch was known for demanding child sacrifice."

Missy and Luisa were silent.

"So, babe, you're basically screwed," ex-Father Marco said in a voice that sounded like Bugs Bunny. It was actually his demon taking over.

"Please bring Father Marco back," Missy said.

"Why waste your time with an intellectual dork like him, when you can have fun with a sexy demon like me?"

"What is your name, demon?" Missy demanded.

The demon made a farting sound. And then giggled like a child.

"Just ignore him," Luisa said. "He feeds upon attention."

"What happened?" ex-Father Marco asked, sounding as if he had just awakened.

"The demon took over," Luisa said.

"I'm so sorry. Was he really bad?"

"The usual," Luisa said.

"Well, since you're still speaking to me and aren't escorting me out of your store, I'll assume there's no lasting damage. So, where were we?"

"Moloch," Missy said. "If this entity is Moloch, how do we fight it?"

"Maybe you should give it what it wants."

"There's no way I'm sacrificing Ronnie."

"Who's Ronnie?" the priest asked.

"A juvenile dragon," Luisa said.

"Sorry, father," Missy said, giving Luisa a dirty look. "I didn't want to get you too deeply involved."

"A *dragon?*"

"To make a long story short," Missy said, "there's a gateway between worlds in the Everglades. The dragons use it themselves but also try to prevent evil entities from passing through. Obviously, they don't always succeed."

"How do they stop the entities?"

"I don't know."

"Well, you need to find out."

"No kidding. Or hope the dragons up their game."

16

MEET MY DRAGON

"We're going to the Early Bird Special at the all-you-can-eat Chinese buffet?" Matt asked through his open window as he parked his car next to Missy's. "Really? Have you been spending too much time with seniors?"

"I thought this was the perfect choice. Not many restaurants serve dinner this early. Remember, I clock in for work at sundown and you were tired of meeting for breakfast," she said, leading the way to the restaurant's door.

Matt had finally gotten her to agree to have dinner with him, and this was the place she chose?

"Just so you know," Missy said. "They have good snow crab legs here."

"And other things easy to eat with dentures, no doubt."

Sure enough, the majority of the people sitting at tables and scavenging through the food stations were seniors. And the place was doing a brisk business at 4:00 p.m.

When they sat down with their food, Matt asked, "Do you

ever wish your patients were just normal old people like these folks, instead of vampires and werewolves?"

"Honestly, no. With the vampires, I can grow attached to my patients without dreading their eventual passing. The werewolves aren't immortal, of course, but they're endearing in the way that supernatural creatures are—the freaks who aren't part of normal society."

"I've always meant to ask you, why can't werewolves go to regular doctors when they're in human form?"

"They can for minor stuff like getting stitches or a tetanus shot. But if they got blood work done it would set off alarm bells. They have distinctly lupine antibodies in their blood that would cause too many questions."

Matt excused himself to make another pass at the food troughs. He didn't understand why women like Missy would go to an all-you-can-eat buffet and only nibble. When he returned to the table, he decided to be direct.

"You've seemed very distracted lately," he said. "Is it because of Schwartz?"

She paused, then nodded. She seemed to be holding something back.

"They just brought out some fresh egg rolls," she said, nodding toward the buffet.

"Don't try to change the subject. I'm a reporter. I can tell when people are holding back on me."

"I'm allowed to have an independent life, you know."

"I'm reminding you of our agreement," he said. "I'll never report anything about your patients or their supernatural goings-on. But in return, you'll accept the fact that I'm fascinated by that stuff and you'll share interesting tidbits with me."

"What makes you think I have any interesting tidbits?"

"You always do."

"You're a very nosy person," she said, though with a smile.

"It's called natural curiosity."

She held her fork idly above her nearly empty plate, lost in an epic internal struggle. Matt, meanwhile, stuffed his face with Chinese noodles.

"The truth is," she said, "I do have a lot on my mind right now."

She looked like she wanted to share her burden. He wisely remained silent while she prepared to lower her resistance.

"You see, my house was attacked the other day by some evil force," she blurted out.

He nodded, as if what she had said was perfectly normal.

"It attacked me because I have an injured creature I'm taking care of in my house."

He nodded and slurped a noodle.

"You promise to keep all of this secret, right?"

He nodded again.

"This creature I'm caring for has a broken wing," she said.

"A bird?"

"No, a dragon."

He finished chewing his noodles. "A dragon?"

"A juvenile one. He's like eighty years old, which is apparently young for a dragon. He's about four feet long, but a lot of that is tail. His family tends to be on the small size, which is actually a benefit when you're hiding in the Everglades."

"I would think so."

"And he's really a dragon, Matt. He's amazing. He even breathes fire. You know how people are always discovering exotic creatures in the Everglades? Well, this one's mine."

"Give me some time to suspend my disbelief of dragons," Matt said. "In the meantime, please explain why an evil force attacked your house."

"It's complicated."

"Of course it is."

"Okay, in the Everglades there's this invisible gateway to other worlds and other planes of existence. Sort of like, 'Scotty, beam me up.' Are you following?"

"Of course I am." He reached for an egg roll and slavered it with enough spicy mustard to open his sinuses and clear the craziness from his head.

"So, for thousands of years, the dragons have used the gateway as an escape hatch, to keep from being driven extinct by humans. They've also been guarding the gateway to keep the evil entity from coming through into this world. Apparently, the dragons have some sort of magical control over how the gateway functions. Make sense?"

"Absolutely. Though you haven't explained yet what this evil entity is."

"I'm not sure what it is. A demon? Ex-Father Marco thinks it's an ancient god. Your guess is as good as mine. The dragon said the entity feeds on children and the offspring of other species, such as dragons."

"Okay, but you lost me at 'the dragon said.'"

"Oh, yes, the dragon can talk. It was raised in Florida, so it speaks English well, with a bit of a country accent."

"Well, duh, what other kind of accent would you expect a dragon to have?" Matt said with maximum sarcasm.

"I would expect an English accent, of course."

"Right. But this isn't J.R.R. Tolkien. This is Florida in the Twenty-First Century. And there shouldn't be any dragons."

"Are you serious?" Missy fixed him with a mocking stare. "Yeah, this is Florida. We have poisonous toads, twenty-foot pythons, cockroaches the size of small dogs, sea cows with propeller scars, and Florida Man. Why would it be odd to have dragons?"

"Good point. Can I see this dragon?"

That caught her off guard. He thought she would have expected him to ask.

"I won't take any pictures," he added.

"I guess you can meet him."

"It's a he?"

"Yes, his name is Ronnie. And before you ask, he was named after Ronnie Van Zant."

"Of Lynyrd Skynyrd? That's so cool I'll ignore how crazy it is."

"You can come by my house in the morning after my shift. I'll call you when I get home."

MATT WONDERED if he should go to a pet store and get a present for the dragon, like he would if going to meet a friend's new puppy. But as far as he could tell, reptiles didn't play with toys. He had no idea what dragons ate, although he suspected meat—including human meat—might be part of their diet. Missy did mention that her neighbor's flowers were constantly eaten by iguanas, so he picked up a cheap bouquet of carnations just in case.

Missy answered the front door just as dawn was breaking.

"Those are for me?" she asked, looking at the flowers Matt held. Their relationship had not yet progressed past friendship to the flower-giving stage.

"They're for Ronnie."

"He's a boy, you know."

"Yeah, I thought he might like eating flowers."

"He's never mentioned it," Missy said. "He does like eating iguanas, though. And mangoes."

"I wish you had told me about the mangoes. I could have brought some."

"So far he's been friendly. You don't need to bribe him."

She led him through the house and into the garage. The dragon was on the windowsill, soaking in the rays of the rising sun.

It really was a freaking dragon.

Just like the fantasy-book images of dragons he'd known since childhood, this creature looked graceful, beautiful, and frightening at the same time. Stout legs, slender torso, power-ful-looking tail, a brontosaurus-like curving neck and a large head with horns on top and on the tip of its nose. One leathery wing was folded atop its torso while the other one was taped. Having medical tape wrapped around it lessened the full high-fantasy effect of its dragon-hood, but Matt was still impressed.

The dragon was watching a basketball game on a tablet. It seemed mesmerized by a closeup of the Orlando Magic's dragon mascot.

Missy cleared her throat. The dragon turned and regarded its visitors. Its dark eyes surveyed Matt with disarming intelligence.

Missy smiled as if she heard a joke. "No, he's not a plumber. He's a reporter. Ronnie, meet my friend Matt."

"Hi, Ronnie."

There was no reply.

"I thought you said he talks," Matt said.

"Ronnie, it's rude to communicate telepathically in front of others," Missy said.

"Sorry," Ronnie said. Yes, those human-sounding words

came from his mouth. "I didn't know we were expecting company. I thought I was supposed to be a secret."

"We can trust Matt. I've worked with him before regarding creatures that needed to remain secret. He's great at reporting and research."

"Ugh," Ronnie said. "Dragons have no interest in that."

"Maybe Matt can help us find your mother."

"Is he your mate?" Ronnie asked.

"Possib—"

Missy cut Matt off. "Absolutely not. He's a colleague."

"I'm still learning about humans," Ronnie said. "You don't seem like a very rational species."

"You seem to be rather fond of Missy," Matt said. "A bit overprotective, maybe."

Smoke began curling from Ronnie's nostrils.

"Don't piss him off," Missy said to Matt. "He's not big enough to bite you in half, but he could easily barbecue you."

Matt took a step backwards. "I can see why you want to save him. He has such a winning personality."

Ronnie belched a burst of flames. The wooden handle of a rake hanging from the wall caught fire.

"Ronnie!" Missy yelled as she grabbed a fire extinguisher and sprayed the rake until it merely smoldered. "We've discussed the rules about no flames indoors."

"Sorry," the dragon said. "I'm a little cranky from getting interrupted while watching the basketball game. I wasn't expecting dogface here to show up."

"The game is a replay from last night," Matt said. "The Magic lost."

More smoke blew from Ronnie's nostrils.

"Thanks for inviting me, Missy," Matt said. "It was a pleasure indeed to meet you, Ronnie. I'll do my best to help her help you. I have to head to work now."

"Let me walk you out," Missy said.

"You have a big heart," Matt said as he exited the front door, "to help that little brat."

"He's a dragon. A *real* dragon. How could I *not* help him? And just remember, dragons and humans are natural enemies, so don't take it personally if he didn't like you."

"He certainly likes you. But how are you going to help him find his mother?"

"We'll look for her in the Everglades, though we don't think she's there. Then we'll try to find the gateway and go through it. And the rest I haven't figured out yet."

"What is on the other side of the gateway?" Matt asked. He was getting frustrated by all the craziness he'd had to absorb.

"I do know it connects to the In-Between, where souls who didn't make it to heaven bide their time. I saw it in a vision once when I was casting a spell. I got a glimpse of the dark entity there, though only a glimpse."

"Wow. It sounds like the gateway is like a wormhole. Maybe it even bridges time. Are you serious about passing through? That could be really dangerous. You may never come back."

"Ronnie has passed through before. He'll guide me."

"Why do you have to go?" Matt asked. He took her hand. "I'm serious. You only need to help him find the gateway and let him pass through to be with his mother."

"It's not that easy. Both he and his mother are being hunted by the dark entity. I doubt she'll be sitting there waiting for him. He'll need some help. And the little bit of protection my magick can provide."

"It sounds too risky to me."

"Part of it is the adventure," she said. "I want to see another world. My curiosity is burning me up."

"If you want to trust a juvenile dragon with your life, that's your decision."

"He's trusted me with his life," she said, withdrawing her hand from his.

"Yeah, and he's a juvenile dragon."

EMBRACING EVIL

Morgan Dreadrick was trimming his nose hairs with his 24-karat gold, diamond-encrusted nose-hair clipper that had been hand-fabricated by an artisan held in one of his private prisons. It had been intended to be a gift to an emir of one of the Gulf nations, he couldn't remember which one, but Dreadrick liked it so much he kept it for himself. He sat on his gold toilet, the clipper in one hand, a gold hand-mirror in the other, when he smelled rotten eggs. And it wasn't coming from him.

A hissing sound echoed within his racquet-ball-court-sized shower stall. The demon Agares emerged from it riding his cantankerous crocodile. Dreadrick was not pleased. It's difficult to negotiate with a more powerful adversary when you're sitting naked on the crapper.

"I didn't summon you," Dreadrick said.

"That's not a very friendly greeting," Agares said.

"Sorry. Welcome to my bathroom while I'm taking care of business." Dreadrick stood up and wrapped himself in a towel.

The crocodile opened its mouth wide at him.

"Just so you know, I can come and go as I wish without being summoned," said the demon. "Now where is the dragon?"

"We haven't caught it yet. But we're close." Dreadrick began to sweat nervously and his right ear, reattached by an expensive plastic surgeon, suddenly ached. "You're not going to hurt me, are you? We're putting every effort into granting your request."

"I might hurt you."

"Hey, would you like to have a vampire? My gift to you to prove my good faith."

"Why would I want a vampire?"

"Do you collect exotic creatures?"

"I collect souls, that's all. I'm a demon. I don't have hobbies and I don't have shelves to display porcelain gnomes or whatever it is humans collect. No, I take that back. I am going to begin collecting the severed body parts of Morgan Dreadrick."

Dreadrick involuntarily touched his right ear to make sure it was still attached.

"You must capture the dragon right away. My master will soon return to the earth after being absent for thousands of years. Already, he has made brief inroads but hasn't crossed over fully yet. When he does, if my gift of the dragon isn't waiting for him, he's going to be really angry. You don't want to piss off a god, especially one that enjoys human sacrifices."

"Who is this god?"

"His name is Moloch. Trust me, you don't want to meet him. Get me the dragon."

The crocodile hissed, and then it and Agares vanished from his bathroom.

On the contrary, maybe Dreadrick *did* want to meet Moloch. An actual god—way more powerful than this lame demon who removes body parts without giving him a single drop of power in return. Why did he need Agares as a middleman?

He searched the Internet for information about Moloch. The ancient Canaanite deity demanded the sacrifice of children by fire. In *Paradise Lost*, Milton even portrayed him as a member of Lucifer's leadership team in Hell who wanted total war with God. You couldn't get much more evil than that.

Moloch could be his ticket to the big leagues of sorcery and evil. And, most important, immortality.

Morgan Dreadrick, a god among men, and Moloch, a god straight out of history. It would be a match made in Hell.

But first, he needed the damn dragon to appease Moloch, because he wasn't prepared to sacrifice any of his revenue-generating prisoners to the god. He would have to lean more heavily on Bonnard to find the elusive reptile and perhaps hire additional investigators. Whatever it took. Then the tricky part would be convincing Agares to introduce him to Moloch.

Dreadrick smiled and returned to trimming his nose hairs.

MORGAN DREADRICK HADN'T ALWAYS BEEN a cartoonish villain. In fact, for much of his life he was simply a dweeb. He wasn't very self-aware, but even he would admit that one factor made him what he was today: love, or, rather, the lack of it.

Morgan's father was a rich, ruthless private-equity corporate raider who bought troubled companies, sold off all their assets, fired their employees, and then sold off the shell of what remained. His only religion was the law of the jungle and the only virtue in his eyes was amassing wealth and power. His father's role models had been the robber barons of the previous century, but those tycoons had feigned an interest in art and culture which Henry Dreadrick despised.

The moment it became apparent that the young Morgan was the intellectual, introverted type was the moment his father despised him as well.

Being born into privilege turned out to be a handicap for Morgan in his father's eyes. The coddled life of nannies, private tutors, and a household staff who treated him like a prince only made him soft, his father believed. Henry had created an origin myth for himself that made it sound like he was born on the streets and fought his way to the top armed with nothing more than his cunning, his grit, and a rusty pocketknife. It wasn't true; he was raised comfortably by an accountant and school-teacher in Long Island, but his real past had been replaced by the origin myth.

Morgan's mother wasn't much help at protecting her son from Henry's bullying and verbal abuse. Nor did she love her son enough to make up for the lack of love from Henry. She was too self-centered to love anyone other than herself and the life of wealth that Henry guaranteed. She was the daughter of an old-money Palm Beach banker, so she grew up soft, too. Henry only married her as his ticket into Palm Beach society. And when he realized that Morgan was not going to be the son he wanted, he divorced her and married a B-actress who would produce heartier stock.

Morgan grew up unloved, except by one nanny, the only one who didn't think he was a spoiled brat. In truth, he was a spoiled, bitter, spiteful brat, because he not only resented his parents for their lack of love, but he also blamed himself. He was the type of kid who'd kick a schoolmate in the shins and then hide behind the teacher, blaming the other child for the altercation.

At least he did receive the very best education. And, when his father's private equity firm became more focused on venture capital, Morgan got large cash handouts to fund whatever cockamamie start-up ideas he had. When Henry's patience for losing money on his son began to grow thin, he suggested Morgan go into the private-prison industry and funded the new company.

Morgan's spiteful personality was a perfect match for this business. The key was convincing state legislatures that a private company would be much more efficient than the state in running each prison. And if he received a contract, he would slash expenses and salaries, so the state paid less and he made more. The human casualties of his business model actually made him happy, because his self-hatred spread into his hating humans in general. Especially convicted ones.

At this stage in Dreadrick's bitter, cynical life, wholeheartedly embracing evil wasn't out of the question. What finally pushed him over the edge was a series of events in a town in Kentucky that was the site of a small state penitentiary. The town was, of course, completely dependent on the prison to supply jobs and use local vendors. The problem was, the crime rate was going down nationwide and there were fewer and fewer prisoners here. Prison workers were laid off and the state prepared to shut the prison down.

Enter Morgan Dreadrick.

Dreadrick Worldwide proposed running the prison, rehiring the workers, and filling the cells with prisoners from the company's other facilities. At a dear cost, of course. Dreadrick demanded that the town and state shower him with incentives, including tax credits and subsidies that nearly bankrupted the town.

It was a bad deal for the town. The restored prison jobs would be at only half the pay, so few of the laid-off workers could accept them and scores of poorly trained workers from other towns filled them instead. Rather than hiring local businesses to supply food and other services, Dreadrick used out-of-state contractors and inmates were served rotten food crawling with bugs. Inmates began dying from medical neglect and malpractice. Three roasted alive in a transport van left in the sun for an entire day. More than sixteen prisoners escaped due to incompetent guards.

But it was a good deal for Dreadrick. His company reported record profits.

Dreadrick went from being the hero who saved the town to the most-hated man alive. Everyone in town denounced him, from preachers to politicians to people on the street. Fortunately, Dreadrick was rarely there because he considered the town to be a backwoods hellhole. Then there was the public hearing about the locals' desire to cancel the prison contract.

When it was Dreadrick's turn to speak, he was interrupted at the podium by numerous catcalls. After he warned the town would face economic devastation if his company left, the crowd began chanting:

"Evil greed! Evil greed! Evil greed!"

An older woman got in his face, screaming, "You're evil!" Spittle sprayed from her mouth. She was completely demented. But something about her reminded him of his mother.

He saw the hatred and contempt in their faces. These stupid hicks hated *him*? He was vastly superior to them in every way and here they were spitting at him? It was ridiculous and wrong. They had no idea how misguided they were.

You call me evil? I'll give you evil, he vowed. He decided that if being a good businessman and job creator would be called evil, then he may as well embrace evil.

Who knows, he reasoned, being evil might be good for the bottom line. And, so far, it turned out that it was.

UNEASY FEELING

M issy drove down the same dirt access road in the Everglades National Park where she had found Ronnie. It was early in the morning, but the sun had risen enough to banish the mosquitoes to the shadows of the low trees that lined each side of the road at the edge of the wetlands. The dragon was with her, perched like a dog in the passenger seat, looking out of the windshield with his hind legs on the seat and his forelegs on the dashboard.

They were so focused on finding the gateway, with not much hope they would do so, that they only had vague plans of what to do should they succeed. Missy had sprayed Ronnie with questions before they left her house. Where would they end up if they passed through? Was there any way to control where they went? Would they just search randomly for endless miles wherever they landed?

Ronnie had admitted that he was no expert at this world-jumping. He had always been with his mother when he passed through the gateway and this was the first time they'd been separated. He said he hoped to make contact with his mother telepathically and get guidance from her.

"Have you communicated with her since you were separated?" Missy had asked.

"No," he said in a low voice. "But I get vivid images of her from time to time that I'm certain she's sending me. It's how I knew she had lured the dark entity away from us."

"So if you're not able to connect with her when we pass through the gateway, then we're toast?"

"Maybe."

"You're not very reassuring," she said.

But she had quickly put Ronnie in the car and taken the turnpike south to Florida City. She felt too much urgency to sit around making careful plans. The dark entity could come back for them at any moment. Or it could be close to harming Ronnie's mother. She reluctantly admitted to herself that many of her bad moves in life had resulted from impulsiveness. But she couldn't help it.

"We're near the spot," Missy said, studying the dirt road in front of them. "But you're saying the gateway might not be here anymore?"

"Yes. It moves around. Sometimes it disappears for short amounts of time. Occasionally there's more than one at different locations at the same time. The elder dragons know how to find them, and even relocate them, but that's beyond my skillset."

"Then why did you want to come to this place again?"

"We have to start somewhere," he said. "I hope we'll get lucky."

"But it can be anywhere? There's no way we can cover every bit of the Everglades."

"It's supposedly attracted to places with lots of earth energy. Whatever that means."

That gave Missy an idea. Perhaps a spell could help find the gateway. At the very least, she should be able to locate points of high energy and narrow down the areas they would need to search. Or the gateway itself should be a vortex of high energy and she might be able to find it directly.

"I know I've asked you this before, but I'm still unclear as to how we're supposed to recognize the gateway."

"You'll get a strange sensation, an uneasy feeling. Most creatures will instinctively move away from it. But force yourself toward it, even as your fear increases. You'll see a shimmering in the air when you're very close and glimpses of things beyond."

"This is going to be difficult. I feel uneasy all the time. Even when I'm on medication."

"It's an existential uneasiness. With anxiety."

"You just described my typical day."

Ronnie remained silent. Missy didn't believe dragons appreciated sarcasm.

"I think this is the spot where I found you," Missy said, stopping the car. She recognized a tall, dead cypress tree at the edge of the water where the road curved slightly. "I don't feel abnormally uneasy."

Ronnie fiddled with the door latch. She leaned over and helped him, pushing the door open. He hopped out and scampered around like a terrier trying to pick up a scent. He trotted farther down the road, stopped, scanned the horizon in every direction, then continued down the road. Eventually he returned to the car.

"I don't feel it anywhere near here," he said.

"What if it's out there?" she asked, pointing at the expanse of water punctuated by tall grass and small islands of trees.

"We'll have to get wet. I can usually feel it even when I'm far away and I don't think it's in this area."

"We'll have to rely on magick, then."

Missy didn't have a particular spell in mind since she didn't fully understand what the gateway was and how it worked. But if there was one thing she did know, it was how to seek out energy in order to harness it for her magick. We all have energy within us, but Missy had inherited a gift from the parents she never knew: an unnaturally deep wellspring of power that she was learning more and more how to tap into. Angels, demons, and other supernatural entities had power that some sorcerers leveraged, but not Missy.

The greatest sources of power came from deep within the earth and out in the universe, the kind that crystals and spell craft draw upon in a very minor way. With her gifts and training, she was attaining more access to the full strength of this power, like finding a main river as opposed to drinking only from the trickle of one of its distributary streams.

Therefore, she was somewhat confident she could tell if there was a major source of energy nearby, whether it be a ley line, fault line, thermal spring, or an energy she didn't understand.

"I'm going to see if I can find the gateway or at least areas where it could be. I'll be back."

She walked back down the road, away from Ronnie and the car. She found a smooth spot beside the dirt wheel ruts and sat down cross-legged. She surveyed the immense blue sky and the scudding cumulus clouds. A flock of egrets flew far overhead like white confetti. She immersed herself in the buzzing of insects and the wet, peaty odors of the land around her. She closed her eyes and chanted a simple string of sounds to clear her mind and calm her heart. In the warmth of the Florida sun, she slowed her breathing and allowed her sense of self to fade away.

Her mind now empty, she became one with the earth.

The Everglades, teeming with life, with water flowing above and below the ground, was also full of power. There were too many scattered pockets of energy to count. They spread for miles around, from the mangrove swamps at the edge of the Gulf of Mexico in the west, to the grass flats of Florida Bay in the south, to the Florida Keys in the east, and through the limestone marl beneath it all.

She sensed major wells of power deep within the earth in this part of the peninsula. There was one nearby, but it confused her. It came from below the earth, but she also felt it in the sky. It seemed to stretch forever in both directions—a very unstable power. In her vision, she saw that it was at the edge of a beach on a point that formed part of an upside-down U. Giant driftwood logs on the sand were bleached almost white by the sun and salt.

The conscious part of her mind reawakened and told her:

It's the gateway.

It took some time for her to return to the here and now. She stood and walked with stiff legs back to her car where Ronnie perched on the hood sunning himself and watching her.

"You should be more careful not to expose yourself during the daytime," Missy told him. "Someone could be hundreds of yards away observing you with a telephoto camera lens or binoculars. We're not in a totally inaccessible part of the park."

He jumped off the hood and crawled beneath the car.

"I'm not that familiar with human technology," he said, "but I get your point."

"I think I saw where the gateway is."

His head popped up and hit the bottom of the car. "Where?"

She described the beach, the gentle, milky green water of what she assumed was Florida Bay, the shape of the point that jutted into it.

"That's Mosquito Point, as humans call it," Ronnie said. "A dragon with healthy wings could fly there pretty easily. It might be a bit harder for us to get there, though."

That was an understatement. Missy studied some maps, which were on paper, fortunately, since Internet service was almost non-existent. Then she drove nearly an hour southwest through the park to Flamingo where there was a campground, marina, and visitor center. At the marina she found a concession that rented canoes and kayaks. Since she expected a lot of wind on the bay, she selected a kayak.

"Gotta return it by five," the skinny woman at the counter said. "Can you get back that soon?"

"Can I rent it for more than one day?"

"You got a camping permit?"

"Yes," she lied.

She finished the transaction as quickly as possible and got the kayak into the water in a canal off the bay. Then she brought Ronnie from the car, wrapped in a beach towel, and placed him inside a hatch in the boat so he wouldn't be seen. After his experience trapped in the burlap bag on the night she first found him, he was not happy about this treatment.

Also in the kayak's hold were water and snacks she bought at the marina. She had no idea how long they would be looking for the gateway.

"Can we take the snacks with us through the gateway?" she asked Ronnie before she stowed him away.

"I wouldn't know. Dragons don't normally carry snacks

around with us. We don't have pockets, if you haven't noticed. We snack on whatever, or whomever, we find along the way."

She didn't belabor the point because they had a long way to go before it got dark. She placed a paper map of the park in her lap, folded down to show their immediate area, and pushed the kayak away from shore. As she paddled out of the protected canal beside the marina and into the expanse of Florida Bay, she had to paddle into the wind coming from the east. She realized this trip was going to be a lot harder than she had imagined.

The water of Florida Bay was the milky-green color she remembered from her vision, but there was a slight chop. Her arms were getting tired awfully quickly. The mainland was on her left, the point she sought was about eight or nine miles ahead of her, and all around were tiny keys covered in mangroves. The water was shallow, and sometimes the bottom was visible, either light-colored sand or dark patches of seagrass. She saw only a couple of boats, far in the distance.

Instead of making a beeline to Mosquito Point, she hugged the land to her left as the coast curved inward to stay in the lee of the wind. Still, there was enough breeze to push the kayak backward every time she paused to rest. Her map said she was in Snake Bight. Lovely name. While she struggled to paddle forward, herons and egrets watched her from the shallows, no doubt annoyed by her trespassing and amused by her stupidity. Her arms burned and she already had blisters on her hands. It had been a long time since she last went kayaking and her muscles were paying the price.

A thumping came from the plastic hull.

"Let me out of here," said Ronnie in a muffled voice.

"I think there's a hiking trail nearby. Someone might see you."

"I'm claustrophobic. Let me out."

"I thought dragons lived in caves. How can you be claustrophobic?"

The acrid stench of burning plastic met her nostrils despite the stiff breeze. Part of the kayak's deck near the bow appeared to be wrinkling and sinking in.

"Okay, stop that, I'll let you out."

She leaned forward, in danger of capsizing the boat, and unclasped the straps holding the hatch closed. It popped open and Ronnie's head appeared facing her. He was angry.

"You are cruel," he said.

"If I'm so cruel, why am I the one doing all the padding with arms about to drop off due to exhaustion?"

"I would have flown here by myself if my wing wasn't broken."

Missy stopped paddling and the boat drifted backwards. "We're running out of daylight and we're only about halfway there."

"I have really good night vision. I'll guide you there if you have the strength to keep going."

Missy closed the hatch to prevent water from splashing into the hull and Ronnie perched atop it. She paddled over toward land until the kayak ran aground and stopped moving. There she drank water and ate an energy bar. Ronnie lapped up water from a cup and ate a few pieces of beef jerky. The sun was low in the sky, with light flaring over the of tops of the mangroves that lined the shore of the bight. With her paddle, she pushed the kayak backward until it was floating freely and continued the eastward paddle.

By the time she passed Porpoise Point, it was dark but in the moonlight she could see a line of land running across their path. That must be Shark Point. It was the left side of the upside-down U that enclosed Rankin Bight; the other side of the U was their destination, Mosquito Point.

And speaking of mosquitoes, the night had brought them out in swarms along with no-see-ums. They buzzed around Missy's head, landing on her face, neck and any exposed skin, though not all of them bit her. She had sprayed herself thoroughly with insect repellant a few times today, but the mosquitoes didn't seem to mind.

Suddenly, fire shot from Ronnie's mouth. He turned in a circle on the bow, spraying the fire like from a flame thrower.

"What are you doing?" she asked.

"What do you think? Killing mosquitoes. You need to move farther from land so they'll thin out."

She did what he said and soon the mosquitoes and no-see-ums went away.

As they approached Shark Point, she saw a light flickering about a hundred yards out in the water from its end.

"That doesn't look like a boat," Missy said.

"It's a chickee, a platform built for camping," Ronnie said. "Four humans are on it."

"Wow, your senses really are sharp."

Fortunately, it was too dark for the campers to see Ronnie. But rounding the point brought the kayak close enough to land to attract mosquitoes again.

"No torching mosquitoes, Ronnie."

He grumbled the dragon equivalent of a curse but held back on his flame thrower. Leaving Shark Point behind, she paddled across the open water of the bight until a dark line appeared on the horizon. It was Mosquito Point. They passed the tiny black hump of Otter Key on their left, indicating they were halfway across the bight.

Her fingers and toes tingled, and adrenaline coursed through her veins.

She sensed a gigantic source of raw earth energy ahead. They finally found the gateway.

Ronnie perked up. He, too, sensed the gateway.

"Do you feel what I'm feeling?" he asked.

"Yes. It's very close. I think it's at the very end of the point."

The excitement of nearing their goal gave her extra energy and she paddled faster. She turned the kayak to the right, aiming it at the point.

"Don't land too close to it," Ronnie said. "That would be dangerous."

She adjusted her paddle strokes to turn slightly left. Soon they were close enough that she could make out the shapes of mangroves along the shore of the point. She didn't see any proper beach. She sprayed herself with bug spray again and then paddled hard.

"Get back here with me," she said to Ronnie.

Once he was sitting in front of her seat, she rammed the kayak into the barrier of stilt-like mangrove roots forcing her way as close to land as she could get. Branches scraped the hull and Ronnie ducked. She used her arms to fend off the branches that tried to slap her face. Finally, the kayak ground to a halt.

Ronnie scampered over the roots and along branches like a squirrel and disappeared into the darkness. She had to squeeze between branches to get off the kayak and then stumbled among the roots as her sneakers squished through the muddy bottom. She found solid ground and grabbed branches to help her climb up to where it was flat.

Then she passed into a large, sandy clearing partly covered in coarse grass and small shrubs. She didn't see Ronnie, so she turned to her right and walked toward the end of the point. For some reason, she felt it would be a bad idea to call his name out loud. So she tried out this telepathy thing.

Keep going, his words appeared in her head. *I'm near the trees.*

She walked further and then saw him. He'd never looked quite like this before. He stood with his hind legs slightly bent, his back arched, head held high. His tail twitched back and forth sinuously. The moonlight glinted off his scales. He was a magnificent dragon, not the docile house pet he had seemed like back home.

The gateway was very near. She didn't see anything, but sensed the energy and felt uneasy and anxious like Ronnie had described before. She wondered if that emotional effect prevented unwary humans and animals from getting too close and stumbling through the gateway.

Ronnie was preoccupied, so she didn't get too close. She stood and watched him until he turned to face her.

"I contacted my mother," he said. "She told me to stay away from her because the dark entity was on her trail."

There was a hurt in his voice that Missy had never heard before.

"Dragons are solitary creatures as adults," he continued. "I never knew my father. But my two sisters were killed years ago when they were young by the dark entity. I became very close to my mother after that."

"I'm sorry," Missy said.

He turned away and continued staring at the trees. Suddenly he ran forward and disappeared.

"Oh, no, Ronnie!" Missy yelled, instinctively running toward where she had last seen him.

The air in front of her shimmered. Her hair crackled as if from static electricity. Fear gripped her stomach, but she kept running toward what now looked like a waterfall with a cave behind it, glistening and sparkling with unnatural light. And then she was too close to stop as a force drew her forward like suction and she entered the maelstrom of colors, strange pricking sensations erupting all over her body.

And then she was falling . . .

. . . face-down onto the hard sand of a beach. She was close to mountainous sand dunes that lacked any sort of vegetation. And opposite them the beach stretched forever to a sea that was barely visible and extended up and down a featureless shore-line. The sky was uniform gray with no clouds or sun. She stood and brushed the sand from her chin, hands and knees.

She was in the In-Between again. But this time, she was here physically. And the realization of that was terrifying.

19

BUGG AND SHUGG

It was early evening and Bugg turned off the engine of his airboat. The boat settled in the water and drifted gently into a wall of sawgrass. It was beginning to occur to him that the roar of the aircraft prop engine was probably scaring away the critters he was trying to hunt. He did enjoy the sensation of skating over all sorts of terrain, over shallow water, over mud, over patches of dry land, and over the occasional kayaker or two. Maybe his older brother, Shugg, was a better hunter because he didn't use an airboat.

Bugg Spencer had been overshadowed by Shugg his entire life. Shugg was bigger, meaner, and more talented at catching and killing critters. Shugg was a little bit smarter, but in their world that didn't matter. Bugg had always lost to his older brother when wrestling and fist-fighting, except the time that Bugg brained him with a two-by-four. Bugg caught fewer gators and pythons. And had fewer wives—just two while Shugg had been on his third.

All those years of rivalry. All the attempts to win the affection of their fishing-guide father who ran boatloads of drugs through the Ten Thousand Islands. Until he got locked up and died in jail from a freak accident involving his mullet haircut and an industrial laundry machine. All those years of believing he hated his older brother, and now he was as weepy as a little girl.

Bugg missed Shugg more than ever. He was determined to avenge his brother's death. How he was going to find the exact python that strangled his brother didn't matter. All he knew was that the Burmese python species was going to pay the price.

Then there was the strange lizard his brother had photographed and had obviously distracted him enough to let down his guard with the snake. There was a big price on the head of this lizard. Bonnard, the man who had pretended to be a journalist and was actually a private detective, promised he'd give him twenty grand for the lizard dead, fifty grand alive. That was enough for a kickass new pickup truck.

He detected movement in the corner of his eye. It was the S-curve of a large, swimming snake. A python. He pulled his Smith & Wesson from the back of his jeans and prepared to send the python to Hell.

20

THE IN-BETWEEN

O ne thing that was distinctly different about physically being in the In-Between was that Missy didn't feel the presence of any souls waiting to go to heaven like she had when she had visited here by enchantment. It felt as if it were a place on earth, though somewhat nightmarish and unlike anywhere she had ever been or seen photos of. There was no sign of Ronnie, or any creatures for that matter, not even a single bird.

She also sensed the lack of the earth power her magick made use of. She had her own organic power inside her, but her ability to cast spells and affect the material world would be greatly curtailed.

The worrisome thought occurred to her that Ronnie might not even be here. He could be in a different In-Between of his own imagining, on a different world, or even in a different dimension.

She felt a lump in her side pocket. It was an energy bar. Turns out she was able to bring snacks after all, at least if they were on her body. She should have carried some water. She wasn't thirsty now, but that could pose a big problem if she couldn't find any here.

Another big problem: She didn't sense the gateway nearby. Logic said that it should be right next to where she landed in this place, but it wasn't. So how was she supposed to return home? She had followed Ronnie through the gateway without thought, an impulsive, instinctual action like a mother would have done to protect her child. Now she sincerely regretted it.

"Ronnie!" she shouted. "*Ron*-nie!"

She didn't know which way to go to search for him. The expanse of beach was empty, so she looked for a place where she could cut through the sand dunes to whatever lay beyond. She had the urge to walk with the dunes to her left, though she had no idea which compass direction that was.

Soon she saw footprints on the pristine sand and was filled with hope. The prints looked like they were made by reptile feet with claws. A curving line in the sand between the footprints sure looked like it came from a tail.

She followed the tracks as they angled up a dune until a low point between dunes appeared. The tracks went through here, still ascending between two higher dunes until they reached a peak and began going downhill. She gasped in surprise.

On the other side of the dunes was a giant rainforest stretching as far as Missy could see. She had gone from a dead landscape to one teeming with life. As she progressed closer to the forest, birds and insects appeared with a cacophony of chirping and buzzing. She was hit by the humid, spicy scent of blooming flowers and trees.

At the base of the dunes a narrow grassy area served as the transition to the forest's solid wall of trees, ferns, and vines. The tracks ended at the edge of the grass. She continued forward, following where the grass seemed to have been disturbed. But once she entered the forest, she would have no way of tracking Ronnie.

A violent shaking of trees and snapping of branches exploded in the forest somewhere ahead of her. She stopped in her tracks, her heart pounding. The sound continued and the tops of trees twitched about a hundred yards in.

Another loud snap, a sharp cracking, and then rising above the forest were giant leathery wings beating the air. A horned head upon a snake-like neck came into view, and she gasped as a full-grown dragon emerged from the treetops, loud thumps against the air with every wing stroke. Once it was fully clear of the forest, it flew rapidly above her toward the dunes and over them.

Her hands were shaking with adrenaline. Was it fear or wonder that was transfixing her? It was a mixture of both. She sat down in the tall grass and waited while butterflies danced above nearby flowers.

It seemed like a long time later, but just as she predicted, Ronnie came walking out of the forest toward her. When he spotted her, his tail twitched and he bared his fearsome teeth in what may have been a reptilian smile.

"I saw my mother," he said.

"So did I. She's gigantic!"

"And fearless. She assured me she's all right and promised to get me when it's safe. But I have to go back to Florida, she said, until the dark entity is off our trail."

Missy was disappointed. She thought reuniting Ronnie with his mother was the best thing to do, ending her responsibility. And, frankly, she wanted nothing more to do with the dark entity.

Ronnie said, "She explained to me the entity, Moloch, once

was a powerful god on earth that many humans worshipped, sacrificing their children to his demand. But dragons refused to obey or honor him."

"That's why dragons are his enemy?"

"Yes. And she told me something else," Ronnie said, glancing around and then lowering his head in modesty. "She said it had been foretold among the dragons for generations that one would be born who would restore the power of dragons and lead them to reclaim their rightful place upon the earth. This dragon would defeat Moloch, and other evil gods, forever."

Ronnie seemed to be having difficulty with his mouth.

"That dragon," he said. "Is me."

"Oh," Missy said. "Congratulations."

"Thank you. I'm not sure I'm up to the expectations."

"So, um, is your mother still okay that you're staying with me?"

"Yes, and she's grateful. It's good that you didn't meet her today because she might have eaten you, just out of habit. Don't take that personally—she truly is grateful."

"Okay, so how do we get out of here?" Missy asked. "I didn't see the gateway near where I arrived."

"You shouldn't have followed me to the In-Between. It's too dangerous."

"Thanks for the warm welcome. I told you I was coming here with you."

"I was hoping you would have chickened out. You know I'm not able to defend you and your magick won't be the same here. Heck, it might not work at all."

"Believe me, I know. I have a bit of juice in me, but I wouldn't be able to protect us very well. So let's get out of here. Where's the gateway? I can't help you find it this time."

"Don't worry. Mother told me where it is right now. But we

have to hurry before it moves."

Missy followed Ronnie along the same track they had taken over the dunes. Once they reached the beach, rather than return to where Missy had arrived, Ronnie travelled with the dunes to their left. The coastline was ruler-straight, so there were no distant points of beach jutting out toward the sea. It was just a straight swath of hard white sand stretching to the horizon.

There was no sun to move in the sky and Missy couldn't tell how long they walked, but she became very thirsty. She wished she'd tried to bring some water with her through the gateway. She didn't bother complaining to Ronnie. They kept walking in silence.

She couldn't resist asking, "Are we there yet?"

"We're almost there," he replied. "I can feel it."

They quickened their pace. She was getting tired and her mouth was parched.

Then the prickling sensation spread down Missy's neck and across her shoulders. The feeling of being watched. She looked around and behind them, but nothing was there.

Thunder rumbled faintly in the distance. Then she realized it wasn't thunder—it was actually hoarse, heavy breathing of some gigantic creature.

"Do you hear that?" she asked.

"It spotted us and it's coming," Ronnie said, stress in his voice. "Here in the In-Between, as you call it, the entity is usually in a physical form."

"I saw it once. When I thought it would kill me. Let's hurry."

They ran. Ronnie's gait was a combination of a horse's gallop and an iguana's scamper.

The ground vibrated in regular intervals, each movement accompanied by a boom. They were the footsteps of the giant god coming from the other side of the dunes. And they were getting closer.

She tried not to panic, but she was about to do so. She didn't notice the unique feeling of unease that came from the gateway, since she was too frightened already, but soon she sensed the energy ahead of them.

They were almost there.

A deep, angry bellow echoed across the sky.

There, right up ahead, the air was shimmering. Ronnie dove through with Missy right behind. Again, it felt as if needles were pricking her entire body. Her stomach lurched as she fell . . .

. . . and landed clumsily on a dirt road, sprawled out in a wheel rut. It was night, though she didn't know if it was the same night she had left before. The heat, humidity, and mosquitoes were oppressive, so she knew right away she was back in the Everglades. She stood and looked around. She recognized where she was: the same place she had originally found Ronnie tangled in the sack.

There was a rustling in the weeds and Ronnie appeared.

"At least we weren't dumped in the middle of the ocean," he said. "That happened once to a dragon I know."

Missy was not pleased. Her car was several miles away at the Flamingo marina. The kayak she had rented was ten miles away from there, stuck on a deserted point of land reachable only by water, with her credit card set to rack up late fees until the boat was returned.

And there was one additional problem.

Blinding headlights flicked on and blinded her. A man stood in front of his truck, about twenty feet away, silhouetted by the light.

He aimed a pistol at them.

21

THE LIZARD IS HUNGRY

onnie froze like the proverbial dragon-in-the-headlights, even as the man approached them. Not only did the man carry a gun, but he had a long pole with a loop of rope at one end. When he got close, Ronnie snapped out of it and darted off into the undergrowth. He didn't make it far. The man lunged at him with the pole, yanked on the rope, and pulled Ronnie out with his neck ensnared.

Fortunately, Ronnie didn't fight back or launch flames at the snare. He knew the man had a gun.

"Careful with him!" Missy said. "He has an injury."

"Of course," the man said. "I get paid more if he's alive." He pointed the gun at Missy again. "Now get in the truck."

The man dumped Ronnie into a large plastic box on the bed of the pickup truck and locked it. He gestured to Missy with the gun.

"I said get in the cab."

She slipped onto a bench seat with torn upholstery, a pile of empty Mountain Dew bottles, and the acrid stench of body odor. The man got behind the wheel and the smell of body odor doubled. He grabbed her wrists and wrapped a plastic zip tie around them.

"If you want the lizard, what do you need me for?" Missy asked. She didn't want to use the word "dragon," but she was afraid the man already knew what Ronnie was.

"Oh, I'm sure I can find some use for you, darlin'," the man said with a leer. His breath reeked of tobacco juice. He wore a camouflage shirt and denim jeans that didn't contain his massive belly. Below his tiny pig eyes were chubby cheeks and a pug nose. Beneath that was what appeared to be a gray-speckled Hitler mustache. Missy examined it more closely. Or was the Hitler look the result of a really sloppy shaving job? The rest of his face hadn't been shaved in several days.

He put the old truck into gear, and it lurched down the dirt road.

"I can't believe you were in the first place I looked for you," he said.

"I can't believe it either."

"How did y'all get out here anyway?" he asked. "Where's your car?"

"We took Uber."

The man snorted derisively.

"My name is Missy," she said. She wanted to humanize herself so the creep would find it less easy to hurt her. "What's yours?"

"Bugg."

"Like an insect?" she asked and immediately regretted it.

"No, it's got two g's."

"It's a nickname?"

"It's my God-given name. It's short for Bugger."

"Of course. Where are you taking us?"

"That's none of your business, darlin'. All you need to know is—dang!" He slammed on the brakes. "If you get out of the truck, I'll shoot you."

Bugg jumped out of the cab, slammed the door, and disappeared. Loud splashing came from the swamp not far away. Missy debated grabbing Ronnie and running away, but she believed Bugg's threat. Besides, her hands were bound by the zip tie and they were on an elevated road running through wetlands. Where could they go except the swamp? And if Bugg didn't pick them off the gators would get them.

A gun fired. Missy dropped her thoughts about escaping. Maybe she could cast a spell to help them.

Bugg was talking to himself as he returned to the truck. A gigantic snake was draped over his shoulders. The truck shook when he threw the heavy snake into the truck bed. He opened the door and got back in, smelling even worse than he had before.

"Wouldn't be surprised if that was the same dang python that killed my brother. Wouldn't be surprised at all. Now it's in Hell where it belongs and I'm going to get some cash for it."

"That's a Burmese python?" Missy asked.

"That is a dead Burmese python. And many more will follow it, believe you me."

"I'm sorry about your brother."

"At least Shugg died doing what he loved. Hunting snakes and other critters." He reached to the floorboards and searched through the trash until he came up with a warm, half-filled bottle of Mountain Dew. He offered it to her.

"Uh, no, thanks."

He took a swig, then burped. "'Scuse my manners. I'm not used to being around people."

Missy wasn't surprised.

He wiped his mouth with the back of his hand. "Now, that lizard you was with—Shugg found it first. He took pictures of it and wrote on his social media post that it was a dragon. But dragons don't exist."

"No, of course they don't," Missy said. "They're just a myth."

"I think that lizard distracted him, so the snake was able to strangle him. The damn thing is partly to blame for his death, in my opinion."

"You don't know that for sure."

"I know that the lizard is going to pay for it one way or another," he said, slamming his hands on the steering wheel.

In her frightened state, Missy couldn't think of any spells that would simultaneously stop the truck safely, immobilize Bugg, and free her wrists.

BUGG PARKED the truck in front of a cheap motel in Florida City. Big Al's Liquors and Deluxe Suites clearly wasn't part of a chain, but the sign out front promised "clean towels and HBO."

Bugg raised his shirt to remind her he had a pistol jammed between his belly roll and his wet jeans.

"I'll be able to see you here from the front desk, so don't try nothing."

He went inside and spoke to a male South Asian clerk who followed Bugg's gaze each time he turned to stare out at Missy. Bugg paid with a wet roll of cash and returned with an old-school motel key hanging from a green plastic disc with the room number printed on it. He drove the car to a spot at the end of the two-story building. After he parked, Bugg pulled out an ancient cellphone from the truck's center console and walked Missy at gunpoint to the room.

While Bugg was unlocking the door, a naked man wearing a Richard Nixon mask and carrying an unsheathed Samurai sword walked by, waved at them, and went into a nearby room.

"Friendly feller," Bugg said. "Must be a local."

Inside the room, Bugg turned on a light and pushed Missy into a rickety desk chair. He left the room, returning with the plastic box that held Ronnie, placing it in the closet area next to the bathroom. He then dropped onto the bed with a shrieking of bedsprings and punched a number into his phone.

"Yeah, I was supposed to call this number. Tell Bonnard I've got the goods and I'm in Florida City at Big Al's Liquors and Deluxe Suites, room one-twelve. Yep. Okay, thanks."

He ended the call. "Guy said not to swim in the pool here if you don't want to get a crypto infection."

"I wasn't planning to," Missy said. "Who's Bonnard?"

"A private investigator. He's gonna pay me for the lizard. He'll come by first thing in the morning."

Missy groaned inwardly at the thought of spending the rest of the night here.

"How about letting me go?" she asked. "You have the lizard. You don't need me."

"How come you were with the lizard?"

"I'm not *with* the lizard. I just happened to be near the lizard when you found him."

Bugg squinted as he stared at her. He wasn't buying it.

"You're a witness," he said. "A kidnapped witness. You could get me in trouble."

"A witness of what? You captured some invasive-species lizard and then gave me a ride to town. No problem. So, you can let me go now."

"You're mighty pretty," he said.

He smiled and patted the mattress next to him as if she

were a dog he wanted to jump onto the bed. A stain was spreading on the bedspread from his swamp-water-soaked jeans. Missy couldn't stop staring at his uneven Hitler mustache.

"May I ask why you trim your mustache like that?"

"It best suits my facial features," he said.

A loud rustling came from the plastic box where Ronnie was imprisoned.

"He's hungry," Missy said.

"Who cares?"

"What if he dies? I thought you said you wanted the lizard alive."

"I thought you said you didn't know this lizard. So why do you care?"

"I don't want any animal to suffer. And what about me? I need to eat, too."

"We'll get something to eat later. Right now it's time for some games."

"If you try anything with me, I'll mess you up," she said in a low voice.

Missy tried to resist panicking. She began casting a protection spell around herself. She really needed to learn some offensive spells. Her personal code of avoiding using magick for harm seemed pretty inconvenient right now. She was capable of tossing objects around through her powers of telekinesis, but there wasn't anything dangerous in the room to throw at him. She'd have better luck trying to hit him with the chair she was sitting on. After a lifetime of being a nurse, hurting people was not her preferred tactic.

She thought of another route, though it made her squeamish.

Bugg laughed. "Mess me up? In your dreams. But I ain't

gonna hurt you. You ever walk on a naked guy in your bare feet?"

"Say what?"

"All you got to do is walk on my back while I'm lying on the floor."

"That's all?" she gave a fake laugh.

"Maybe that's just the beginning." The way he leered at her sickened and resolved her.

"How about this," she said. "You feed the poor lizard before he starves to death and then I'll play your games."

She pulled the energy bar from her pocket. It was pretty squashed at this point.

"Feed him this. When these lizards are hungry, you never know what they'll do."

Bugg didn't argue. He was too excited anticipating his little game. He grabbed the energy bar and brought it to the closet.

"Dinner time!" Missy said.

Bugg opened the box containing Ronnie.

And his head was immediately engulfed in flames. He shrieked and Ronnie let out another blast of fire.

Missy yanked the wet bedspread and doused the flames as best she could with two hands tied together. Bugg groaned with pain. Ronnie climbed out of the box and prepared to attack again.

"Help me here," she said to him and he bit through the zip tie around her wrists.

Her hands freed, she used one of the extra zip ties protruding from Bugg's rear pocket to tie him up, though it was a struggle as he writhed on the dirty carpet.

"Calm down," she said. "I'll help the pain."

She cast a quick, simple analgesic spell she normally used when she had migraines. It wouldn't last long, but the paramedics should arrive soon. She took Bugg's truck keys from the dresser and left his gun out in full view for the police to find. Then she called 911 on the room phone and reported that a meth cooker had experienced burns.

"Goodbye, Bugg. Don't bother us again," she said as she slammed the door behind her.

"Gosh, it smells in here," Ronnie said when they got into the truck.

"We won't be in here for long."

Missy drove a few blocks to a gas station where she parked the truck and left the keys under the front seat. Ronnie had to submit to being wrapped in a rain poncho she bought at the convenience store. She used the payphone to call a cab and during the long wait for it, and the even longer ride home, she contemplated the impossible odds of not only being with a dragon, but a dragon that was wanted by both a dark entity and a private investigator working for an undoubtably malevolent client.

She couldn't imagine a more dangerous predicament to have. But in her experience, fate always found a way to ratchet up the danger in her life.

22

THE SUMMONING

Driving home from errands late one afternoon, right before reaching her driveway, something flashed in front of her car and Missy slammed on her brakes. It was Ronnie trotting across the street from her neighbor's yard carrying an iguana in his mouth. She sighed as he made his way up her driveway and around the garage.

This was unacceptable. Ronnie couldn't be allowed to risk being seen like this. Maybe in the past someone could have mistaken him for yet another iguana if they saw him at a great distance. But Ronnie had grown since she'd been keeping him, thanks to resting and eating well. Now he was larger than the biggest iguanas and it would be difficult to mistake him for anything other than a dragon.

After parking, she went around to the side of the house where Ronnie was devouring the iguana beneath the open garage window he used for access. He alternated between cooking the flesh with bursts of flame and eating it as savagely as a lion dining on a wildebeest. She had to look away.

"Ronnie, you can't go running around the neighborhood like this. You're going to be seen."

He was polite enough to finish chewing before he answered.

"You drove all the iguanas off your property. What else am I supposed to do when I'm craving chicken of the trees?"

It was true. She had gotten fed up with the iguanas eating her flower and vegetable gardens, so she devised a spell to ward them off. But that removed Ronnie's main source of prey aside from the occasional squirrel. (She had made him swear not to eat any of the cats that occasionally wandered onto the property.)

Her neighbor across the street was completely overrun by the invasive lizards. His house was on a freshwater canal, which attracted iguanas, and there were always several sunning themselves on the sea wall and his pool patio. His gardens were completely destroyed, and to add insult to injury, the iguanas pooped in his pool. In Ronnie's mind, he was doing the neighbor a favor by eating the pests.

"Look, I've tried eating squirrels and other rodents. Too much effort for too little meat. Can you come up with a spell that summons iguanas back to your yard?" Ronnie asked. "Only at mealtime. And only the plumpest ones."

"I'll see what I can do."

Spells to ward off or repel creatures vary from protection spells that create an invisible barrier of force, to those that affect the will of a creature and make it recoil when it tries to come to you. Summoning spells, however, are more like the latter. Only the most powerful witches or wizards can force a sentient creature to move against its will. Most witches use a summoning spell to convince a creature that it wants to come to you and direct it how to do so.

It is actually more difficult to summon a living creature than a demon or departed spirit, because they can get to you directly without navigating city streets. And they most likely have been summoned before, so they know the drill. Unlike living creatures with strong willpowers.

Missy consulted her grimoire, or, as she called it, her "Cracker Magick Recipe Book." She combined details from a couple of spells and burned incense made from a potpourri of local herbs. Since this spell was new to her, she wanted the extra power of kneeling within a magick circle on her kitchen floor. She lit five equally spaced candles to represent the four elements plus the fifth element of aether, or, spirit. Then she chanted the words in ancient Greek, the meaning of which she had no idea.

Bubba strolled into the kitchen. The cat knew better than to interfere with her spell casting. He sat watching her. Just as she was finishing the spell, he lunged at an ant nearby.

"Bubba! You just broke the magick circle!"

He didn't seem concerned. She didn't have the sense that the spell was disrupted.

Afterwards, she waited for the results. She looked out of every window and didn't see a single iguana, not counting the carcass of the one Ronnie had eaten earlier. Sometimes spells don't work the first time you try them. Or the second or third or fourth time, for that matter. She was going to have to convince Ronnie to eat hamburger instead.

Hours later, she heard Ronnie calling from the garage.

"Missy!"

She walked through the laundry room and poked her head in the garage. "What?"

"Look out the window."

Her lawn had disappeared. Instead it was a giant, shifting

mass of brown and green flesh. Every inch of her property was filled with iguanas, large and small, thousands of them. More iguanas than she had ever seen in her life combined.

"Oops," she said.

"Oops?" Ronnie said with a sarcasm that was not in his nature. "I appreciate the easy pickings, but don't you think this will attract unwanted attention?"

She went to the front of the house. The mass of iguanas not only covered her entire lawn but also spread out onto the street and onto other lawns. Neighbors were gathering to gawk. The iguanas closest to the people ran away, but circled back around to rejoin their brethren. Additional stragglers showed up from other yards and even came rambling down the street.

She realized she'd better do something before the TV news trucks showed up.

A crash came from the garage. She ran across the house and looked in. Four large iguanas ran around in a panic, a couple of them knocking over garden tools as they climbed the walls to avoid Ronnie.

"I'm collecting a herd of them," he explained.

She went back to the kitchen and looked at her grimoire to figure out what to do. A banishing spell? The warding off spell she had used before?

The annoying notes of "Pop Goes the Weasel" drifted into the house and grew in volume. Apparently, the ice cream truck had been repaired after it ended up in the tree. Instead of filling her with joy and thoughts of sweet treats, the truck and its loud, cloying music annoyed her, especially since she slept during the daytime. She hoped that no kids came running after the truck. That would make her iguana invasion even more of an issue with her neighbors.

"I wish the iguanas would take out that damn truck," she muttered out loud.

Suddenly, a giant rustling sound came from outside. And the pitter-patter of tens of thousands of tiny clawed feet.

A man shrieked in horror.

She raced to the living room window and beheld the sight of the ice cream truck engulfed in iguanas: on its roof and hood, clinging to its sides, stuffed into the open windows, long tails hanging out. The truck slowly rolled to a stop, squashing some iguanas along the way. The neighbors who had come out to watch Missy's problems were all shooting video of the attack with their phones.

The truck swayed back and forth, then appeared to rise slightly before moving backwards down the street, back from where it had come.

The lizards were literally "taking out the damn truck."

Missy had created an army of iguana zombies that were enslaved to her will. Her spell had gone way beyond what she had intended.

"Cool," she said.

As the ice cream truck disappeared around the corner, she realized what she had to do.

"Iguanas, return to where you were before I summoned you," she commanded in a loud voice, even though they clearly didn't need to hear her voice with their ears.

Small groups of the lizards ran in different directions down her street, each going to a different lot, more favoring the homes that were on the canal. In a few minutes, everything was back to normal.

"Um, excuse me," Ronnie said as he walked into the living room. "I know you don't like me to come into the house, but—"

"Don't use my words against me. I don't want you to clash with the cats."

"I wanted to let you know the iguanas I was herding just escaped."

"I sent all the iguanas back to where they came from. Luring prey to my yard for you just isn't going to work out. I'd feel uncomfortable using my magick to help kill critters, anyway. I removed the spell that warded them off. You're going to have to prey upon only the ones that show up in the yard or go hunting elsewhere only at night when you can't be seen."

Ronnie was not happy. He stomped out of the room (as much as a lizard could stomp).

A DAY LATER, Ronnie showed up in the living room again while she was lying on the sofa reading a book.

"Um," he said, "I think your spell is still working."

She sat up quickly. "Oh no. Another horde of iguanas?"

"No. It's anoles. But something is different. Stand outside of the garage window and see what I mean."

She went outside to the side of the house. Near the garage window she saw only a few anoles. The tiny green lizards, similar to geckos, were perched on a low stucco wall that protruded from the side of the house. One of them tried to gain attention from a mate by pulsing out a disc of skin under its throat.

From inside the garage, Ronnie climbed onto the windowsill and looked around.

The anoles suddenly jumped to attention and stared up at Ronnie. More appeared out of nowhere, joining their colleagues on the low wall while others clung to the wall of the house surrounding the window. There were dozens and dozens of them.

But it wasn't a flood of lizards like the iguanas summoned by her spell. She guessed this was simply the normal population that lived in her yard. And the anoles weren't acting enchanted or under any unnatural influence. They gazed at Ronnie with rapt attention, as if he were a rock star.

Ronnie raised his front leg in a friendly gesture. The anoles crouched and lifted their bodies back up like a pushup. She'd seen lizards make that motion often but not all in unison.

"It's like they're worshipping you," Missy said quietly.

"I get the same feeling," Ronnie said. "You know, anoles are among the smartest of reptiles."

"Don't be so quick to compliment yourself."

"I'm serious. It's as if they know about me."

"I wonder if somehow they sense what your mother said— about you being the chosen one."

"She meant of the dragons," he replied.

"But aren't the dragons the king of reptiles? They know you're a superior species and that there's something special about you."

He lowered his leg then raised it again. The anoles made the same crouching gesture. Almost as if they were genuflecting.

"I think they *are* worshipping you," Missy said. "As if you're a king. Or a god."

"I only wish the dragons I know would treat me with this kind of respect."

"Maybe they will now. Maybe something is changing in you as you grow older."

"It's too much to understand right now," he said as he prepared to climb back into the garage."

"I hope you don't take advantage of this and eat them."

He gave her a dark stare. "I would never do that. Besides, they don't have enough meat on them."

That hadn't stopped her cats from eating the occasional anole, but she didn't mention it. It seemed sacrilegious now.

23

BELOVED MUSTACHE

Bonnard received the call from out of the blue. He had been feeling defeated after that cretin, the snake hunter, failed him. The cretin, Bugg, was in the emergency room vowing to catch the dragon again and to get revenge on the woman he had captured with the dragon, but it was too late. Bonnard thanked him and gave encouraging words, but he was done with that moron.

Therefore, it was such a pleasant surprise when one of the animal trappers he had contacted previously called.

"Hey, this is Frank from Acme Trappers. I remembered you were asking about lizards that looked like dragons. Well I was trapping some iguanas at a house in Jellyfish Beach and sure enough, I saw this really crazy looking lizard. It was hunting iguanas. It ran across the street with an iguana in its mouth and disappeared behind a house. I went looking for it, but I couldn't find it. Man, it really did look like a small dragon. For sure. And it wasn't a Komodo dragon, that's a fact. I've caught a couple of them before."

Bonnard wrote down the address and thanked the man. So the dragon was living in a home, no doubt belonging to the woman Bugg had mentioned. He found it odd that a civilian would take in a dragon. Did she think it was a pet? The cretin had said the creature looked injured. Why would the woman nurse a dragon back to health?

Dreadrick hadn't explained why he wanted the dragon. Obviously, he wasn't the only one who wanted it. Bonnard might have to increase his finder's fee.

But first, it was time for a little trip to Jellyfish Beach.

BONNARD HAD no moral qualms about killing the woman. And he was pretty good at murdering people, cleanly and without leaving any incriminating evidence. But inevitably the police would get involved and it was best to avoid that in this case.

That's why he staked out the house for an entire day. He didn't see the dragon, but found an iguana carcass that had been devoured under the open garage window. Parking in different spots around the neighborhood, he observed the woman's comings and goings. Once she left in the late afternoon, it appeared as if she may not return for a while.

After it was completely dark, Bonnard parked his Porsche in the woman's driveway. He had to do this job quickly even though he'd never kidnapped a dangerous animal before. To be honest, it was beneath his dignity. He was an expert at capturing criminals and making political dissidents disappear. He wasn't a lowly vermin trapper. But there was no time to find a replacement for the injured Bugg. He briefly considered enlisting the trapper who had tipped him off on the dragon, but didn't trust the man to keep a secret.

Bonnard wasn't even sure of what techniques he should use, but he took from his car a blanket, a roll of duct tape, and a coiled section of rope—the basic ingredients for securing a captive. With no time to spare, he headed around the side of the house directly to the open window. Before climbing in, he shined his tactical flashlight through the window. He didn't see the dragon amid all the typical garage clutter, but it could be hiding. He pushed his gear through the window and climbed in.

He stood in the darkness and waited for a few minutes, listening. No sounds of movement. He clicked on the flashlight and searched the space thoroughly, from floor to ceiling, opening cabinets and boxes, looking under tables. He saw a pile of blankets arranged like a nest where the creature probably slept. An unfamiliar, spicy scent came from the blankets.

The dragon wasn't in the garage. Bonnard swore under his breath. He couldn't afford spending all night searching.

The interior door leading to the house had a cheap handle lock that Bonnard popped easily with a screwdriver without causing any visual damage. He passed through a laundry room and then into a hallway. He avoided using the flashlight so neighbors wouldn't see it through the windows.

Tiny claws clicked across the hardwood floor. He jumped and shined the flashlight at the sound. The glowing green eyes of a cat stared at him from beneath a couch in the living room. He clicked off the light, angry at himself for being startled.

The search of the house went quickly. He didn't want to disturb anything and give away that the house had been searched in case he needed to return here and search again. Mostly, he just looked under furniture and inside closets. All he found was a second cat who was not happy to see him.

Bonnard returned to the garage. The dragon must be out hunting or something. Was it worth his time to wander the neighborhood searching for it? As he stepped onto the concrete floor his eyes were drawn to the garage window.

The dragon was sitting on the windowsill, looking at him.

Bonnard froze. The dragon was a good fifteen, twenty feet away. If he lunged for it, the dragon would bolt out the window. He wished he had a tranquilizer gun. Maybe he should just shoot it with his Beretta and hope that Dreadrick would accept a dead dragon.

"It's okay, little dragon," Bonnard said in a soothing voice.

The dragon cocked its head. Bonnard inched a little closer to it and paused. The dragon didn't move. So he moved a couple of feet closer. Still, the dragon remained on the windowsill watching him. Bonnard moved with baby steps one more time. When the dragon didn't respond, Bonnard lunged.

Tossing the blanket over the dragon, Bonnard wrapped his arms around the—

The force of the blast of fire knocked him backwards and the pain made him scream. The blanket was on fire and on top of Bonnard who flailed about on the floor to get it off him.

As soon as he got the blanket off, the dragon landed on his chest, its face inches from his own.

"Please don't burn me."

Instead, the dragon bit half of Bonnard's nose off.

Bonnard knocked the dragon off him. His first instinct was to escape, but he forced himself to tackle the dragon. The duct tape was on the floor nearby and the rope was in his back pocket. He realized that neither were very effective when you didn't have any hands free.

As he pulled the rope from his pocket with his right hand, the dragon wriggled out of his grasp. It stepped back and released another blast of fire.

Bonnard ran back inside the house, slammed the door, and

rolled on the floor to extinguish his burning clothes. The door somehow popped open. The dragon shot out of the garage and bit Bonnard on the ass. He screamed and ran blindly down the hall. He made it to the guest bedroom, closed the door, and locked it.

How did he let this happen? Bonnard asked himself. Poor planning, that's what. He should have hired the trapper to catch the dragon and then killed the trapper afterwards to make sure he didn't talk. His mentor, the police chief of Gonaives, had always told him the most important part of an operation was guessing beforehand everything that could possibly go wrong.

He opened the door a crack. A brief burst of flames slipped through the opening, enough to singe the door but not catch fire. He quickly closed it.

The damn dragon was holding him prisoner in here. What was he supposed to do? He caught a glimpse of himself in a mirror mounted atop a dresser. His nose was nothing but a gaping wound, his eyebrows and his mustache—his beloved mustache—were gone, and his clothes were in tatters. Fortunately, his burns didn't look that bad, although they hurt like hell.

He weighed calling an associate to rescue him, but didn't like how that would play out for his reputation. Instead, he pulled out his Beretta and blew two holes in the door.

He cautiously opened it, hoping to see a dead dragon on the other side.

Nope. Nothing was there. No blood, either. Bonnard decided to make a tactical retreat and declare the mission a failure. Next time, he'll send a trapper. That is, if there would be a next time. He wasn't sure he wanted to work for Dreadrick anymore. The guy was kind of a dick, was always late on paying his invoices, and now was responsible for Bonnard losing half a nose and his beautiful mustache. Giving up his reputation as a ladies' man was too much of a price to pay.

He left the room and tiptoed to the home's front door. When he undid the bolt and opened the door, the burglar arm went off. He didn't care. He ran toward the driveway and stopped in surprise.

A car was parked behind his Porsche. The crappy old Toyota was completely blocking his escape. A low brick wall on one side and a hedge on the other ruled out the possibility of driving over the lawn.

In the faint glare from a nearby streetlamp, a person was visible in the Toyota's driver's seat. His Beretta in hand, he walked up to the car and tapped with the barrel on the driver's window.

The driver, a woman with long hair, glanced at him with unconcern and continued to sit there.

"Back your car out," he said, pointing the nine-millimeter at her head, the barrel pressed against the glass.

She stared at him impassively. He was getting really mad. He wanted to shoot her, but knew the gunshot would alarm the neighbors.

"Back your car out, now!"

Still, she didn't move. He tried to break the window with the handle of his pistol, but it just bounced off. It was the oddest sensation—as if there was an invisible layer of plexiglass covering the window. He pounded the window a few more times with no effect, the vibrations jarring his wrist and elbow.

"I don't need this crap," he said.

He aimed at the top of the window, away from her face, and fired a round.

Nothing happened. Except a sharp pain in his left cheek. Blood ran down his face and over his neck. He touched the wound before he finally understood that he had just shot himself with the ricocheted bullet.

And one of his gorgeous, high-angled cheekbones was shattered.

What would the ladies think of him now?

24

INTRUDER

Missy's racing heart began to slow down after the protection spell successfully deflected the bullet. The truth was, she hadn't been sure it would, especially at close range. Her magick was still fairly new to her and she was far from confident that anything about it was guaranteed.

She had been drawing a blood sample from a vampire patient in his Squid Tower condo when she heard Ronnie's insistent voice in her head:

A man broke into your house. He's trying to capture me.

She immediately cut the consultation short and drove home. Her first instinct was to call 911, but she worried about having the police wandering around her home and yard and spotting Ronnie. If the intruder managed to catch him, and the police then caught the intruder, they would find Ronnie. She couldn't imagine the chain of events that would then occur except that the events would be bad. She decided to scope out the situation first and see if her magick could help. If all else failed, she would call the police.

If her magick worked, she would be more aggressive. A lot more.

When Missy reached her house, the intruder's silver Porsche was in her driveway. She parked right behind it, at an angle, blocking his escape. She was just finishing her protection spell when she heard the burglar alarm blaring inside the house. Then the alarm-monitoring company called. She gave them her password and told them to hold off calling the police, that she thought it was a false alarm, and that she was nearby and would check out the house.

The tall, handsome black man appeared in her window with a gun and a foul mouth. Well, he seemed handsome at first, but he was missing half a nose, most of a mustache, and both eyebrows.

She concentrated on her spell. *Please, please, please work.*

His attempts to break the window didn't work. She didn't think he would shoot his gun in her neighborhood, but when it became clear he would, she almost panicked. When the bullet ricocheted off the protection barrier and hit him in the cheek, it was time to get aggressive.

She disabled the protection spell, and wove a binding spell around him. He stiffened and sank to the ground, his arms against his sides. She got out of her car and approached him warily, as if he were a dead shark that could still bite. He lay on his side, the windbreaker he wore despite the heat was in charred tatters and revealed the gun tucked in his pants. She removed it and placed it on top of her car.

She studied him. The bullet had gone in and out of his cheek, leaving two bloody holes and some tooth damage. Aside from his wounded nose, he had an assortment of minor burns on his face and neck. Ronnie had done a good job on him. Which gave her an idea. She reached out telepathically.

Ronnie, come to the front of the garage door. I need your help to convince the man to answer my questions. Try to stay out of sight of anyone else.

Soon she heard rustling in the plantings next to the garage and Ronnie appeared.

"Why are you trying to steal my pet?" she asked the man in as threatening a voice as she could muster.

Pet? I'm no one's pet!

Play along with me, Ronnie.

The man didn't answer her.

Pretend you're going to eat the rest of his nose, she said in her mind.

Ronnie crept up to the man's face and roared. She'd never heard him do that before and it scared her, too.

"Get it away from me!" The man sounded traumatized. He wriggled, but couldn't move any more than that.

"Then answer me."

"I'm just a private investigator. I was hired to get the dragon."

"Who hired you?"

"I can't say."

Ronnie put his face inches from the man's.

"Please make it go away!"

Ronnie's creepily human-like tongue tickled the man's bloody stub of a nose. The man gave a low-pitched whine and struggled against his invisible binds.

"Tell me who hired you and I'll save you from my pet. The thing is, he's really hungry."

The man whimpered.

"And he likes to cook his meat before he eats it."

Ronnie blew smoke from his nostrils into the man's face.

"But I can't—"

A small ball of fire landed on the nose-nub. The man shrieked in panic.

"His name is Morgan Dreadrick. Some super-rich CEO. You can't touch him."

Ronnie's head shot up in alarm before he bolted around the side of the house. At the same moment, a car pulled up in front of her driveway.

It was a Jellyfish Beach Police SUV. A short African-American woman in uniform got out. A second police unit pulled up behind her.

"Your neighbors reported a dispute and a gunshot," the officer said.

"I interrupted a burglar," Missy said. "He was trying to make me move my car so he could escape."

A second officer, a burly male, joined the first one and they approached the prone P.I. Missy undid her binding spell just before they reached him. Sensing he was unbound, he scrambled to his feet and started to run before the first officer executed a perfect cross-body block, knocking him back to the ground, before jumping on him and cuffing him.

Missy had to retell her version of the story several more times before they finally left with the intruder. She didn't even have time to relax before she realized that she and Ronnie were going to have to go into hiding now that their location was known.

"I'D LOVE to have you guys as houseguests," Matt said when she called him and explained what had happened.

"I'm sure you would. But I need to be able to see my patients easily so I'm going to stay at Squid Tower. It's also safer for us with so many vampires in close proximity."

"I never thought I'd ever hear anyone say that."

"That is, if they allow pets."

"I'm not a pet," Ronnie called from the garage. "I can hear you out here, you know."

"The reason I called was to give you a name," Missy said. "I managed to get the private detective to tell me who hired him. Have you heard of Morgan Dreadrick?"

"My God! Are you serious?"

"Yes. Why?"

"That's the CEO of the company that runs the prison camp where I think your vampire friend is being held."

"He's not my friend," Missy said.

"That's such a crazy coincidence. It sounds almost as if the guy collects monsters."

While they were talking, Missy clicked away at her laptop in the kitchen.

"I called you right after the police left and I hadn't even looked up his name. I've never heard of him, but I see with all the mentions on the Internet that he's pretty controversial. And looking at photos of him, I'm pretty sure he's the guy who blocked my locator spell with black magic."

The dark hair, thin nose, and weak chin. The self-righteous smirk. It was definitely the face from the image she received when his spell blocked hers.

"You're saying Dreadrick used black magic against you?"

"Yes. I'm sure of it."

"Wow. It's hard to imagine a public figure like him is secretly a sorcerer. CEOs already have enough ways to game the system without using magic."

"What can we do with this information?" Missy asked.

"For starters, I'm going to have a little chat with him."

25

A GREAT MAN'S LEGACY

S hameless flattery was usually enough to convince the gatekeepers that Matt would do a positive story about the important people they worked for, and thus allow him to conduct interviews. It took a lot more work to manipulate the public relations director at Dreadrick Worldwide. Because the corporation and its leader were even less popular than rabies.

Matt hated to admit to himself that it probably was his lack of a track record in investigative journalism that made him seem harmless enough to score the interview. But that was how he managed to get here, sitting alone in a chair beside a low table in the sitting area of the massive office of the CEO, looking at the magnificent view of Miami's shimmering Biscayne Bay nineteen stories below, as he waited for his powerful interviewee to show up.

A door different than the one he had used opened in the dark-paneled wall. A model-thin blonde in a tiny black dress came in, ready for battle. He quickly stood.

"Gretchen White," she said, shaking his hand.

"Matt Rosen. Thanks so much for setting this up."

"Okay, but remember, no questions about prison conditions or migrants. You promised this interview will be a personal profile."

"Of course. I want to learn what made him the man he is today."

"Mr. Dreadrick is such a good man and that's never reflected in the media. It's about time people saw how kind and generous he is."

"You didn't give me a bendy straw!" a man shouted from an adjoining room. "How many times do I have to tell you I must have bendy straws with every beverage? Where is my bendy straw?"

An older-sounding woman apologized profusely in Spanish.

"What is wrong with you? You're fired! I'm calling ICE to deport you immediately. Now get out of my face, I have an interview to do."

Morgan Dreadrick strode into the room, grinning ear-to-ear, which wasn't a long distance in his narrow face.

"Mr. Rosen, great to meet you," he said shaking Matt's hand and patting him on the shoulder. "I've read some of your articles. Great story on that city council meeting about pet waste regulations. Riveting reading."

"Thank you, sir."

Gretchen and Dreadrick sat on the couch. Matt took a chair across the low table from them. An overweight, bald man in a rumpled suit entered the room with three bottles of expensive spring water. He placed them on the table, opened one and placed a purple plastic bendy straw in it before handing it to Dreadrick.

Dreadrick didn't take the water. He cleared his throat ominously. The bald man bent the straw at a precise forty-five-degree angle and only then did Dreadrick accept it. The bald man left in a hurry.

"That's our Chief Operations Officer," Gretchen explained.

"You know, I normally don't do interviews with newspapers as small as yours," Dreadrick said, "but I want to support my community."

"That's very generous of you. And that's the point of the series I'm doing, profiling the leaders and influencers of South Florida to boost community pride. You'll be the first interview."

"Who's the next one after me?"

Matt had no idea, since he hadn't even pitched this series yet to his editor.

"The governor," he lied. "If we can get him."

"You'll get him," Dreadrick said. "I'll make sure of it. I own him. He's one hundred percent bought and paid for. The sniveling little weasel wouldn't be elected dog-catcher if it weren't for the bales of cash I've dumped on him."

Gretchen was making the "cut-it-off" symbol with her hand below her chin. But Dreadrick pretended not to notice.

"I own almost all the politicians in this state. It's the cost of doing business, you see. I need their influence to privatize existing prisons, to give me the contracts for new prisons, to enact laws that make prison sentences longer. That's a lot of cash and dark money I have to lay out."

"Let me know when I can turn my audio recorder on," Matt said.

"Morgan, why don't you tell him about our adopt-a-road program," Gretchen suggested.

"Our what?"

"We're pledging to support litter cleanup of five miles along U.S. 1," she said.

"Okay. I also donate prison laborers for free to my friends for yard work and stuff," Dreadrick said. "Is that considered charity?"

"Let's talk more about you," Matt said, placing his phone on the table between them. "I'm recording now. What personal characteristics led to your success?"

"Thank you," Gretchen said under her breath.

"Good genes," Dreadrick said. "I'm actually a more advanced form of the human species than people like you. More intelligence. Stronger willpower. Greater ruthlessness. . ."

"Your faith," Gretchen said. "Tell him about your strong faith."

"I have very strong faith in myself, my genius at deal making, and the power of my money."

"Your *religious* faith, Morgan. Remember, we discussed that."

"Oh, right. My faith in God is my foundation. God gives me strength and wisdom."

Matt scribbled notes on his pad.

"Good," Gretchen said, smiling.

"And Satan gives me cunning and some very clever ideas."

Gretchen desperately waved her hand beneath her chin.

"I'm very open-minded about religion," Dreadrick said. "I respect all faiths. Diversity in how we worship is what makes America great."

Gretchen smiled. Matt scribbled.

"In fact," Dreadrick continued, "there are many gods that have been neglected or forgotten over the centuries. Gods that have much to offer us if we make the proper offerings or sacrifices to them. The power they can give us—it's just beyond the imagination."

Gretchen appeared to have become seriously nauseous.

"And demons, too," Dreadrick said. "Demons get a bad rap for possessing people. But if you can convince a demon to serve you, man, you can mess up your enemies big time."

Seeing his opening, Matt asked, "Have you encountered any supernatural creatures?"

Dreadrick laughed. "I am like the Number One expert on supernatural creatures. Not only have I encountered them, I have proof they exist." He looked as if he were dying to brag more.

"What kind of proof?" Matt asked.

"We don't have time for such silly questions," Gretchen said. "Why don't you ask Mr. Dreadrick how he built such a gigantic corporation so quickly."

"Yes," Matt said. "It's almost like you have magical powers."

Dreadrick smiled. "Oh, if you only knew. If you only knew."

"Tell me a bit about your personal life. Why is it that such a rich and powerful man is unmarried?"

"My ex-wife cost me a fortune. Why would I go through that again when, for a simple cash transaction, I can—"

"Mr. Dreadrick dates discretely," Gretchen said. "But there is no lucky woman waiting in the wings."

"What's next for Dreadrick Worldwide?" Matt asked.

"Enormous growth. We plan to expand into other industries, but I can't give any details at this time. I'm also trying to arrange a partnership with a very powerful entity. I'm talking scary-powerful. My company will be unbeatable after that," he said with a knowing grin.

"What do you want to be your legacy."

"The fruits of all the great deals I've made. I want to be known for my brilliance, strength, power. I want to be a dominating force in the world and to live forever."

"Your achievements to live forever, you mean?"

"No. Me. I want to live forever. And one of these days I'll figure out how."

Dreadrick stood abruptly to signal the end of the interview and Gretchen ushered Matt from the executive suite.

"He's a great man," she said to Matt, "but don't take what he says too literally. He jokes a lot. And he speaks in metaphors and parables that are too complex for people like us to understand."

"Yes, of course," Matt said, though what he was really thinking was, *This man is nuts.*

MATT MET Missy at the all-you-can-eat Chinese buffet that evening. As he sipped his iced tea, he found himself wishing he, too, had a bendy-straw.

"Well, did you learn anything?" Missy said.

"I learned that he's a raving lunatic. A true megalomaniac. He did say he had proof that supernatural creatures exist, though he didn't specify how."

"Like if he is holding a vampire prisoner?"

"Nope. He didn't say."

Missy nibbled on stir-fried vegetables. "Did you record the interview?"

"Yeah, here." Matt cued up the audio file on his phone and handed it to her and hit play. Missy held the phone to her ear to listen over the buzz of the restaurant.

Her eyes widened at various points of the interview. At others, she snorted with laughter.

"What a clown," she said, returning the phone to Matt. "I

believe he has Schwartz. And I think the reason he's keeping a vampire is his reference to figuring out how to live forever."

"You mean he's doing medical experiments on Schwartz to figure out how vampires can be immortal?"

"Could be. Or a simpler explanation: He wants Schwartz to turn him into a vampire."

Matt shuddered. "The man truly is crazy."

"And what also got my attention was when he mentioned a partnership with a very powerful entity."

"Why? Do you have a stock tip?"

"'Entity' is a very generic word and you'd assume he was talking about a corporate entity," Missy said. "But we've been using that word for evil force that's crossing into this world and trying to attack Ronnie. And what a coincidence, but Dreadrick is going after Ronnie, too."

"You think he's trying to catch Ronnie for the evil entity?"

"Could be. Maybe he believes the entity will give him something in return. Dreadrick loves to say he's a genius at making deals."

"He would have to be a genius to make an enforceable deal with an evil entity," Matt said. "And that makes it all the more important to protect Ronnie. Are you all set with a place to stay?"

"Almost."

"Well, my offer for you guys to stay with me is still standing," Matt said.

"I really do appreciate it. But I'll be staying at Squid Tower," she said, neglecting to mention she hadn't worked that out yet.

"Where's Ronnie now?"

"He's still at my house until I move him to Squid Tower, hopefully tonight. I told the alarm service that I've been under a threat and to notify the police the instant my alarm goes off.

And Ronnie has new rules: No keeping the garage window open and he has to hide in the attic when I'm out. He's not happy, but it's hopefully temporary."

Although she suspected that his living arrangements in Squid Tower wouldn't be much better.

26

DRIVE A HARD BARGAIN

Agares appeared to be a little depressed. If demons could experience depression, that is. He appeared out of thin air in Dreadrick's sorcery room, while the CEO was watching *Wheel of Fortune* on his walls of televisions. Dreadrick switched them off when the demon appeared.

"You're telling me the dragon escaped again?" the demon asked, not as angrily as he would have before.

"From two of my best men," Dreadrick said. "This is not a submissive dragon."

In the past, Agares would have punished Dreadrick with a flesh wound. But tonight, he just sagged with apathy. His crocodile didn't even hiss.

"Moloch is going to come down hard on me," Agares said. "I don't know how I ended up involved in this crap. Moloch is senior to me, of course, but he's never been my supervisor before. Satan has been on this kick about 'corporate reorganization' and it's really stressful for us demons."

"Worry not, my demonic friend. Now we know where the

dragon is staying and who's taking care of him. Even if they try to hide, we will find them."

"Moloch was brutal to me when I told him the dragon escaped from your man the first time. I'm not looking forward to telling him there has been a second time."

"C'mon, have a seat," Dreadrick gestured to a chair across from his at the Incan sacrificial altar he used as a worktable. The demon hesitated, then got up from the crocodile's back and sat in the chair.

"I feel your pain, Agares, but look at it from my point of view. I've lost two men, gravely injured, possibly fatally," Dreadrick lied about the men who were recovering nicely. "I've spent tens of thousands of dollars on this search. And you expect me to follow your orders through threats alone? I have a company of ninety thousand workers who depend on me to feed their families. This company could lose millions of dollars if I have to run around being stupid for you. There comes a point where I must sacrifice my ears—or my life—in order to do what's best for these families."

"The money part is convincing," Agares said, "but I know you don't give a damn about families."

"Okay. Point taken. I want to pitch a deal that's a little more beneficial for me. So I don't just give up and let you kill me—without you getting the dragon and therefore suffering the wrath of Moloch. What a waste that all would be! Bad for me and bad for you."

"Tell me what you're proposing," the demon said with a growl.

"As I mentioned before, I want Moloch to grant me immortality when I deliver the dragon. He's a god. It shouldn't be such a big deal for him."

"Moloch also demands child sacrifices. You have an inexhaustible supply of children at your disposal. It shouldn't be such a big deal for you." Agares smirked.

"Remember those ninety thousand workers who depend on me? I'll lose lucrative government contracts if I sacrifice my prisoners." Dreadrick paused just long enough before adding, "However, if Moloch gives me immortality, and I know it's legit, I will grant his request for sacrifices."

"I'll pass on your request. He won't be pleased, to put it lightly. But you'd better get the dragon. Because if you make a demand like this to a wrathful ancient god and you don't deliver your side of the bargain. . ."

"Gotcha," Dreadrick said, fully confident in his deal-making prowess.

27

THE VAMPIRE'S HOUSEGUESTS

"Of course, you're welcome to stay in my condo," Agnes said to Missy over the phone. "But you do know we have a strict pet policy here? One pet under twenty pounds. But I'll make an exception for you so you can bring both your cats."

"Thank you, Agnes. I've seen very few pets around here."

"Sadly, not many vampires have pets. When you live forever, it's depressing how short pets' lives are."

"Is there such a thing as pets that are vampires? Like dog or cat vampires?"

Agnes said in a solemn voice, "That never ends well."

"I have to mention that there's a lot more to this story," Missy said, pacing nervously around the inside of her house. "There's an additional houseguest I have to make arrangements for. You see, I'm taking care of a dragon."

"A dragon?"

"Yes, a juvenile one. Not too big. Very polite. Potty trained. Doesn't make a mess. He's why I can't stay in my house."

"You have a lot of explaining to do," Agnes said.

Missy obliged. She went through the entire tale, from finding Ronnie, to the attacks by the dark entity, to their journey to the In-Between. Then she described the private investigator's breaking into her home, and his connection to the man who was most likely holding Schwartz prisoner. Missy could tell that Agnes was sympathetic to her cause.

"Even though vampires are supernatural creatures, we don't know everything that's going on the supernatural world," Agnes said. "Just like anyone, we get caught up in the minutia of our daily existence. And there's no *Supernatural Weekly* TV show to keep us up to date on what is going on. So, frankly, I'm amazed and heartened to hear that there are dragons still in this world."

"Yeah, and they protect us from this dark entity and Lord knows what else."

"Keeping him out of the hands of that twisted man who has Schwartz is important in itself," Agnes said. "My three-bedroom condo is too big for just me, so you and the cats will be fine. But it sounds like your dragon might not enjoy being cooped up inside."

"No, he won't."

"I have an idea. The entertainment facility next to the swimming pool has a kitchen and bar that we never use, of course. He could stay in there. There are sliding security shutters closing off the bar that we can prop open slightly, just enough for him to squeeze in and out of."

Missy opened the door to the garage and gave Ronnie a thumbs-up.

"Thank you so much, Agnes. We'll be there tonight."

BUGG HAD BEEN SITTING in his truck parked a block from Missy's house for an hour after she drove past him and into her driveway. He hoped she didn't recognize his truck. He seethed with anger at her for rejecting his amorous advances and tricking him into the ambush by the dragon. The burns on his face still stung as they slowly healed.

But as pretty as she was, she wasn't going to distract him this time. He was going to stay focused on his mission of getting the dang-blasted dragon.

Bonnard had called and given him the woman's address. He said he got busted for breaking into her house and bonded out, but had some injuries he didn't want to talk about and needed Bugg to follow up. Bonnard had warned that she probably wouldn't stay at that address for long. If, by any chance, she did, the dragon would be in the garage. Bugg was hesitant to break in, given what had happened to Bonnard. He wanted to have a better idea what the woman was up to.

Without turning his headlights on, he moved his truck a little closer to her house. All the lights were on inside and he could see her moving from room to room. She made frequent trips to her car in the driveway, carrying suitcases, a couple of boxes, and two crates for small animals.

Finally, the lights went out. And she carried something large wrapped in a blanket to her car.

The dang-blasted dragon.

She was obviously moving to a new place, which was good news for Bugg. She'd be much more vulnerable now, at least until she hunkered down in the new place. He put his truck into gear and followed her car at a distance. It was shortly after midnight and traffic was light, so he'd have to be careful not to be spotted by her.

He followed her along residential streets and then onto

Jellyfish Beach Boulevard. She went east, crossed the Intra-coastal bridge, and then headed south on A1A. Finally, she pulled into the entrance of a condo tower on the ocean side. Bugg noted the name of the place—Squid Tower—as well as what the building looked like and kept driving. The guard at the gate would never let him in, but he would park somewhere and see if he could slip onto the property by foot.

He passed a public beach and a small strip center. After making a U-turn, he parked at the strip center in front of a closed ice cream shop. Then he walked north on the beach until he recognized the building looming on the other side of the sand dunes.

There was a sign on the wooden dune crossover that said, "Squid Tower residents only. No trespassing." Bugg ignored it and went up the stairs. He sat on one of the benches at the end of the boardwalk structure. Moonlight illuminated the incoming waves on the ocean, and he pretended to watch them while he stole glances at the property to look out for security guards. No one was around.

At the west end of the dune crossover was a large swimming pool with a single-story building next to it. There were a few lights around the pool complex, but plenty of shadows. He was surprised to see his quarry walking past the pool. Missy was carrying the bundle wrapped in a blanket. She went inside the building.

Bugg couldn't believe his luck. Now he knew exactly where to search. And this time he was better prepared. Under his shirt was a tranquilizer-dart air gun he had bought online.

28

SPECIAL OPS

I t was another emergency meeting of the Squid Tower Homeowners Association Board of Directors. And, Agnes sensed, the mood was grim. She sat at the center of the table with Kim, Bill, and Gloria.

"Our attorney has hit a brick wall," she said. "None of the Homeland Security agencies can find any records that they have Schwartz, and she is getting stonewalled by Dreadrick Worldwide, which owns the prison we're pretty sure does have Schwartz. She has filed a lawsuit against them, but that could take a long time to work its way through the courts."

"Then what can we do?" Kim asked.

"We go in there and rescue Schwartz ourselves," Bill said.

"You and what army?" Kim asked sarcastically.

"An army of vampires, like me and the many of us that own firearms."

"What do you mean by, 'the many of us'? Vampires don't need firearms to kill," Kim said.

"We just like to collect guns, okay? Spend some time at the shooting range. It's fun."

"Let's show some common sense," Agnes said. "We can't launch a violent assault on the prison. That's completely contrary to our laws of anonymity and self-preservation. The prison guards would see us being unharmed by their bullets, and if a single one of us were killed by fire or decapitation, or arrested, our community would be revealed."

"Then what do you suggest?" Bill asked in a petulant tone.

"We somehow sneak him out of there. It will require cunning, misdirection, and lots of mesmerizing of the guards."

"And weapons," Bill said. "Just in case. It's better to be prepared."

Agnes sighed. "Bill, after this meeting let's gather you, Oleg, and Sol. We'll start planning an operation."

Bill pumped his fist in victory.

The board meeting soon broke up, and while Agnes waited for the amateur special-ops team to arrive for their meeting, she wondered if she was making the right decision. She knew that trying to free Schwartz was a great risk, but leaving him in the possession of the humans was even riskier—not just to the fate of Schwartz but to that of all the vampires.

The saving grace was that if Schwartz was being held secretly, and there was no paper trail of him, he was probably just as much a secret to much of the staff at the prison. There probably weren't many guards assigned to him. Missy had said she believed him to be in a separate compound at the prison. The security undoubtably would be high, but a surgical strike had a better chance of working than if they had to attack an entire prison.

Even the senior-citizen vampires of her team could over-power guards and jump over fences. Well, Oleg, at least, could jump fences. The others could probably only climb stairs. At least Missy would have some magick up her sleeve that could add to their stealth and confuse the guards.

As if on cue, the door to the meeting room burst open and Missy rushed inside.

"Agnes, they've taken Ronnie."

"Calm down, child. What happened?"

"The pool kitchen was broken into, the door smashed open. And Ronnie is gone. I've tried to reach him telepathically, but he won't answer. What if he's been killed?"

"We're going to rescue Schwartz soon," Agnes said. "Maybe the dragon will be in the same place and we can rescue him, too. The prison we believe is holding Schwartz is owned by the same man who you said wants your dragon."

"But how are we going to rescue them? My magick can go only so far. I have a lot of work to do to create a spell powerful enough to take out an entire prison."

"You don't need to," Agnes said, patting Missy on the shoulder with her ice-cold hand. "This will be, as they say, a surgical strike. When the others get here, we'll devise a plan."

THE VAMPIRES AROSE AT DUSK, fed on microwave-heated bags of whole blood, and gathered for a quick pep talk by Oleg before they slipped into a minivan in the Squid Tower parking garage. In command of the party was Agnes, who, despite her body age in her early nineties, still threw a spear better than an Olympic javelin thrower, a skill she was trained in since early childhood as a Visigoth 1,500 years ago. In operational command was Oleg, who had led many a cavalry charge in the wars of Catherine the Great. The "muscle," as it were, consisted of Sol and Bill whose body ages were in their sixties and between them owned more firearms than a small-town police department.

And with them was a single mortal human armed with magick. First, she had to retrieve her Sun Pass toll transmitter from her own car because she was the only one whose account hadn't expired. The vampires also talked her into doing the driving. At least she knew her van-load of senior citizens, since they were vampires, would not need to stop and pee along the way.

They took the two-hour journey south on tollways that skirted the cities and the edges of the Everglades until they reached the bottom of the peninsula. There, the sprawl of South Florida and its tangle of highways petered out into the twin strings of U.S. 1 and Card Sound Road stretching straight through empty wetlands down to the Keys.

The prison was surrounded by farm fields and there was no place close to the fence around the secret compound where the van could park unseen. So they parked in a strip center parking lot not far from the main prison entrance.

As planned, Missy recited a short spell. And they waited for the great migration.

29

IGUANA ARMY

Residents of Homestead and Florida City at first thought the persistent rustling in the trees outside their homes was caused by a windstorm. Then it turned into a sound almost like raindrops drumming on their driveways and the streets beyond. It didn't last long, so they returned their attention to their televisions and digital devices.

In a motel, a tourist from Indiana was waiting for a struggling ice machine to fill his bucket so he could continue on his booze bender. He felt small animals rubbing against his ankles. At first, he thought they were cats, but realized the animals didn't feel furry. He looked down and couldn't see his feet. The floor of the breezeway was dense with green iguanas moving in one steady direction. The man was drunk enough not to panic. He remained stationary, watching the creatures flow by, his brain struggling to process it.

Past the breezeway was the swimming pool. The iguanas at the edges of the mass flowed around the pool while the rest plunged in like lemmings, swam across to the shallow end and climbed out. Two teenaged girls on floats screamed.

"They are on a mission and I can tell it is of sacred importance."

The words came from a naked man carrying a Samurai sword and wearing a rubber Richard Nixon mask. He crouched near the ice machine, holding his sword vertically in front of him, while the iguanas respectfully went around him.

"We are most fortunate to have witnessed this tonight," the naked man told the tourist from Indiana. "It means the gods are smiling upon us."

"Who are you and why the hell are you naked with all these iguanas around?"

"I am Florida Man," he said. Then he nodded as if all had been explained.

People who were out and about town didn't feel as fortunate as the naked guy. One driver slammed on her brakes before reaching what appeared to be a green tsunami flooding the roadway ahead, engulfing the cars in front of her. Only as it thinned out, several minutes later, did she notice the twitching tails and scurrying claws of untold numbers of iguanas.

Some as tiny as a human finger, others as long as a Dalmatian, they all traveled in unison, in the same direction, with frightening urgency.

The woman was so freaked out she didn't even think to shoot any video for social media. Speaking of shooting, surprisingly few people used their firearms on the reptiles. Those who did quickly realized it was a waste of ammunition to try to thin out the throngs.

From Homestead to Florida City, the folks in stores and businesses that were still open heard the eerie rumbling along U.S. 1. People ran to windows to watch, jaws agape in astonishment, as the iguana hordes marched past. They flowed between cars, on top of cars, and under cars with predictable carnage. But the sight of their comrades getting smeared onto asphalt didn't cause any of the reptiles to falter. They were all of one mind to keep moving forward and obey the force in their brains that was stronger than any animal instinct.

From all compass directions they came and joined the main channel of the green river, where the currents flowed both from the north and the south until they met at an intersection, coalesced, and turned onto a street that led east. They passed residential neighborhoods and mobile home parks then crossed under the turnpike. Soon they turned onto a road that lead to the main gate of the prison camp, passing a strip center where a minivan packed with vampires had pulled out ahead of them.

As they neared the prison, Missy turned off onto a dirt farm road while the iguana tide continued to roll onward toward the main gate. She drove onto another road that ran parallel to the prison with a field in between. She continued along the length of the main camp compound until she and her passengers spotted the smaller compound. She parked behind a rusty Quonset hut that was surrounded by weeds.

The team waited until an alarm went off at the main prison. She got out of the van and peered around the corner of the hut using Sol's binoculars that he had liberated from Schwartz's condo. The chain-link fence that surrounded the prison sagged from the weight of iguanas that climbed it. The green mass swirled around the entire perimeter of the main compound, covering every inch of fence. Then they began leaping off in droves into the prison yard.

There were shouts, spotlight beams shifting through the darkness, and, finally, two guards exited the secondary compound, which was unmolested by iguanas, and ran toward the main one. When they neared the iguana flood, they stopped, unsure of what to do.

Missy had to maintain the spell controlling the iguanas, but still spin additional magick. Younger vampires could easily jump over the fence. Her vampires. . . well, it wasn't exactly a sure thing, so she refocused her mind and power and soon the gate of the target compound shifted open, just in case. Oleg, Sol, and Bill jogged inside, Bill carrying a large pair of bolt cutters. Missy followed.

At such close range, her locator spell quickly found Schwartz. She turned it off immediately before Dreadrick could sense her magick.

"He's in this first container," she said.

Bill cut open the padlock with bolt cutters and they all stormed inside.

"What the hell took you so long," Schwartz said sitting on a sleeping bag in the corner.

He was still as ornery as ever, which meant he was in good health. Seeing that Ronnie wasn't in there, she left the container as Bill was cutting the cable that tethered Schwartz to the wall. She called to Ronnie telepathically as she wandered among the other three containers. He didn't answer.

Two of the containers didn't have padlocks on their doors. She looked inside and they were both empty. The one at the far end, however, was locked.

As the team escorted Schwartz from his cell, Missy called for Bill to join her.

"I need you to cut off this lock," she said.

The container was dimly lighted. As her eyes adjusted to the dark, she saw a human-like figure huddled on the floor with a tether on its neck. She approached it, with Bill behind her.

It was a clown. An evil clown.

Its clown attributes were natural, not a costume and makeup. It had a red, bulbous nose, hair in a pink afro, a white face and wide, red lips that looked almost painted.

It opened its eyes—yellow eyes with green pupils—and studied Missy and Bill.

It smiled, baring brown, needle-like teeth, and chuckled with a gurgling, inhuman sound.

"Should we rescue it?" Missy asked.

"Nope," Bill said. "I've always hated clowns."

"Me, too."

They left the trailer, allowing Dreadrick to keep one item in his collection of monsters.

Once the vampire minivan was away from the prison and merging onto the turnpike, Missy released the iguanas from the spell, directing them to scatter and return to their neighborhoods. She felt badly that some of them had died because of her, and she feared that many would have trouble finding their ways home after waking up from her spell. But she reminded herself that they were, after all, an invasive species that was overrunning the Florida she loved, and they would probably be happy to invade any neighborhood with enough food to eat.

Her most pressing concern was finding Ronnie. Why couldn't she communicate with him?

IVAN, the sole employee working the overnight shift in the Homestead convenience store spent every hour praying that he would end his shift without being shot. He'd heard they always assign the new guys to the overnight shift, the explanation being that store traffic was much lighter than at other times and the inexperienced clerk would have an easier time handling it.

But Ivan knew the truth: The new guys were more expendable. So they were put in a brightly lit store in the hours past midnight when nothing else was open and the druggies were coming off their highs and needed money to re-up their buzzes, and when the gang members were driving around with pent-up aggression that needed release. The store was a magnet for trouble.

There was an emergency button beneath the front counter. And a lot of the other night guys carried a weapon (unofficially, of course). The way the laws were in Florida, you were more likely to get out of jail for shooting a robber than for clobbering him with a baseball bat.

Ivan, however, did not have a gun. Having just arrived from the Ukraine, he hadn't known that it was mandatory according to the U.S. Constitution for all citizens to pack heat. At least that was what his upstairs neighbor asserted.

But no one told him about swords. He'd never heard that Americans carried swords as well as guns.

So why was this man carrying a sword into the store?

The man was naked and wore a rubber mask on his head of some jowly old man that Ivan didn't recognize. But, most concerning, the naked man was carrying a Samurai sword. Unsheathed and poised to strike. Ivan's hand felt along the bottom of the counter, searching for the emergency button.

"Do not resist, my friend," the naked man said as he entered, holding the door open behind him. "I command an army and I will show you no mercy if you do not submit."

The naked man was skinny and pale, not tan like many of

the Floridians that Ivan had seen. In his nakedness, it was clear that he was not carrying a gun. The man was also free of tattoos, which was rare among Americans younger than sixty. Ivan's eyes quickly moved to the "army" following the man into the store.

Green iguanas. Dozens of them. Walking into the store as if they owned it.

"You were lost, my little children, you unwitting pawns of a sorcerer. But I have shown you the way," the naked man said to them.

"The way to where?" Ivan was bold enough to ask.

"To the freezers," the naked man said. "There was a near-freeze a few winters back and the iguanas were dropping out of the trees, cold-stunned. You could pack hundreds into your car and they wouldn't wake up for hours."

"I see. You collect iguanas. And why is that?"

"I have a friend in Deerfield Beach who sells iguana meat to customers from Central America. I have been blessed that so many iguanas have come to me. We will get rich."

The naked man was herding the lizards into the ice-cream freezer. They crawled into it without hesitation, moving as if they all were controlled by the same mind.

"Why are they obeying you like that?" Ivan asked.

"I can only conclude," the naked man said, "that they are enchanted by some magic spell that hasn't worn off yet. It is their loss and my gain."

"Okay," Ivan said.

While the iguanas crowded into the freezer, the naked man walked up to the counter. Ivan's hand searched for the button again. But he couldn't find it.

The naked man brandished his sword. Ivan prepared to die.

"Beer," the naked man said, "you will give me two eighteen-packs of light beer in exchange for two iguanas. Two big ones with plenty of meat. Deal?"

"Deal," Ivan said, happy to remain alive.

"They call them chicken of the trees. Great in stews and burritos."

Ivan allowed the naked man to take two eighteen packs from the cooler and to drink several beers while he waited for the iguanas to lose consciousness. While the man packed the cold-stunned iguanas and the remaining beers into plastic bags Ivan supplied from behind the counter, the electronic chimes rang as the front door opened.

A young gang-banger wearing a windbreaker rushed in and pointed a handgun at Ivan.

"Gimme your cash. Now!"

The robber was nervous and repeatedly thrust his gun toward Ivan's face. But he noticed Ivan's eyes roam from the robber's gun to something behind him. The young punk turned his head to see what it was.

But not in time to duck from the Samurai sword about to connect with the back of his neck.

Ivan's hand finally felt the emergency button beneath the counter. He pushed it.

The headlines were, believe it or not, fairly typical for Florida:

"Naked Florida man arrested for decapitating convenience-store robbery suspect. Thirty-four frozen iguanas seized."

The iguanas, by the way, all survived and were released back into the wild. Except for the two that Ivan kept and served in a Ukrainian stew to his in-laws the next day. They didn't realize the stew meat wasn't chicken.

Ivan's request to transfer to the dayshift was approved by corporate a week later.

30

THE DRAGON WHISPERER

Bugg awoke from a heavy whiskey-and-pain-pill sleep lying on his back on the floor of his Everglades cabin. His couch/bed was only six feet away, but that must have been a hike too far last night. He brushed away whatever insect was crawling across his face.

In his half-awake state, he thought the dragon was talking to him. He wished dragons had snouts like alligators that you could tape shut, but there was no way to shut this lizard up so he could go back to sleep.

Bugg's eyes snapped open when he realized that he wasn't dreaming. The dragon *was talking*.

"I said, do you have anything to eat? Meat, ideally." The human words came right out of the dang lizard's mouth.

Bugg rubbed his eyes. His head felt like it was full of peanut shells and hurt like hell.

"Did you talk to me?" he asked the dragon. It felt kind of silly to do that.

"Yes, I talk. Humans aren't the only species that can talk.

You're not even the smartest creatures on this planet. Especially not you."

Bugg slapped his own face twice. It didn't make him feel any more alert. And it didn't make him look any smarter. It just hurt.

"The booze and pills are making me hallucinate," he said.

"You're not hallucinating," Ronnie said. "I really can talk. If you can accept the fact that dragons exist, why can't you accept that we can talk?"

Dang, Bugg was really happy now that he hadn't killed the dragon. After he captured it, he had wanted it to wake up from the tranquilizer so he could watch it suffer while he butchered it. He hadn't cared anymore about getting the fifty grand from Bonnard for delivering the lizard alive. He'd give up his chance for a new truck and take the twenty grand for the dead carcass instead, just so he could make the critter pay for burning him on top of its role in his brother's death.

But the dart must have had a lot of juice on it and the lizard slept for more than fourteen hours. Now that he knew the dragon could talk, Bugg got to thinking. If Bonnard was going to pay fifty grand for the dang thing, it must be worth much more than that. Maybe some fancy zoo would pay double that or more.

And then Bugg got to drinking again from the nearly empty bottle that was still within arm's reach.

Maybe he wouldn't sell the dragon after all. He'd keep it and charge people good money just to see it. He could even go on TV talk shows with it, although he'd have to buy some decent clothes to wear. Maybe some big-shot producer would offer him his own reality show.

His world just became wider now that he knew the dang lizard could talk. It would become the most famous critter on the planet and Bugg would be the most famous critter-handler.

All those jerks who thought he'd amount to nothing would see how wrong they were.

Bugg the Dragon Whisperer. He could already imagine his name on the marquees.

"Um, I'll be happy with a hamburger, even," the dragon said. "But only if it's fresh."

"I'll feed you when I get some grub for myself," Bugg said. "Last time I tried to feed you, you burned me."

He didn't like taking orders from a reptile, even one that was going to make him rich. If Bugg didn't get his own reality show out of this, the dang lizard was going to be dead meat. Literally. He pulled his phone from his pocket.

When Bonnard answered, Bugg said, "I ain't found the dragon. It looks like the lady moved out of her house."

"You've got to keep looking," Bonnard said. He made a whistling sound with each word. "I've got a bunch of problems of my own to deal with right now."

"Why are you talking so funny?"

"I was injured. I told you that before."

"So how am I supposed to find the dragon now?" Bugg asked with feigned ignorance.

"The woman works at a condo on the beach. Look for her car along A1A." Bonnard described Missy's car and gave her plate number. He said he had to get off the phone to make a court appearance for his burglary charge. "But keep looking for the dragon."

When he ended the call, the dragon was staring at him. Like it knew something that Bugg didn't. It bothered him that a lizard thought it was smarter than him.

"Aren't you hungry?" the dragon asked. "Because I sure am."

Bugg was beginning to think he might just kill the dang lizard after all.

Missy changed the sheets in Agnes' spare bedroom before she went to bed. Not that the sheets were dirty. They simply had been on the bed for over ten years and smelled a little musty. Missy figured that retired vampires didn't get a lot of houseguests. No grandkids coming to visit unless their grand-children also happened to have been made into vampires.

The air conditioning was another problem. Apparently, vampires weren't as heat-sensitive as humans and tended to keep their condos rather warm to save on electricity. Missy asked permission to lower the air to 79 degrees.

Everyone was tired after the raid on the prison, so Missy scarfed down some takeout tacos in the kitchen while Agnes "retired" to her bedroom to sleep, even though Missy knew the old vampire rarely slept. Missy set up a cat station in the guest bath where she squeezed a litter box between the toilet and the bathtub, placing their food and water dishes atop the vanity.

Missy settled into bed in the fresh sheets with the cats by her feet. She had no desire to watch TV, especially since the television looked to be about thirty years old. She turned off the light and instantly fell asleep.

Until Ronnie's voice echoed in her head.

Missy, he captured me.

Who took you?

Bugg, that disgusting redneck from the Everglades.

Do you know where you are?

I can't tell. I've been trapped in his cabin, but I can smell the Ever-glades outside. I think he wants to kill me.

I'll try to find you. If you get any clues about your whereabouts, tell me.

Okay.

Stay safe, little one.

Missy sat up in bed, but kept the light off. The tracer spells she sent blanketed Everglades National Park. She waited and when there were no pings, she directed the tracers beyond the borders of the park through Big Cypress National Preserve and to the west of it.

Finally, a ping. It came from near the Ten Thousand Islands, the area along the Gulf of Mexico that was a labyrinth of mangrove islands, twisted channels, and hidden backcountry bays. Performing a quick locator spell on the floor of Agnes' guest bedroom, she found Ronnie. He was in a small cabin near Everglades City.

Now she needed to figure out a plan for how to get him out of there.

31

DESPERATE PLAN

Morgan Dreadrick had just finished berating his CFO for not having an instant answer to how they would overcome sagging revenues for the past two quarters. It was 11:30 p.m. Dreadrick enjoyed calling his C-suite leaders late at night to ruin their evenings and their home-life balance. It kept them on their toes. And it allowed Dreadrick to take out his stress on someone.

Anyway, the CFO should have had an answer to how they would deal with the nation's falling crime rate. That, of course, meant fewer prisoners to throw in Dreadrick Worldwide's prisons and thus lower profits.

"Why don't we simply find a way to increase the crime rate?" Dreadrick asked.

The CFO paused. "But how, sir?"

"Get Congress to make more things illegal. Or maybe there's a new drug we can spread around. A drug that's illegal to possess and that makes people do illegal things."

"I'll look into it, sir."

"Good. I want to see a report on my desk tomorrow."

He clicked off the call. But the phone immediately rang. It was Bullock, the supervisor who was responsible for Dreadrick's Special Collection.

"Sir, I regret to inform you that your newest vampire escaped."

"How?" Dreadrick was fuming.

"Um. . . a party of heavily armed mercenaries broke in and retrieved him."

"How was that possible?"

"Um. . . I'm still gathering data on that."

"What about my other vampires?"

"Um. . . they're gone, sir. Don't you remember? You ordered them staked earlier in the year."

"I know, but I thought I still had one of them left. They were all uncooperative anyway. What about my evil clown? Did we lose him, too?"

"No, he's still being held."

Dreadrick clicked off and tossed his phone aside. What a crappy night. He enjoyed ruining his employees' evenings, not the other way around.

But that was only the beginning of his problems.

He awoke in the middle of the night with the strong urge to scratch his itching right ear. When he attempted to do so, he discovered the ear was missing. The one the demon Agares had removed and the expensive plastic surgeon had reattached. There was no blood, no pain. And no ear.

He groped under the pillows and sheets without finding it. Then he looked under the bed and found a small bundle wrapped in parchment paper. He also found his Boo-boo Bear he had lost months ago, but there was no time for snuggling now.

Kneeling on the rug atop the marble floor (the rug was a pelt of the rare Siberian tiger he had killed), he opened the bundle. There was his ear and a note written in old-fashioned cursive on the inside of the wrapper and signed by Agares.

Moloch is angered by your demands and failure to deliver the dragon. He will appear on earth tomorrow to mete out your punishment.

This wasn't fair. There had to be a way out.

He called Bonnard. "Where the hell is that dragon?"

"I think Bugg took it for himself."

"Who the hell is Bugg?"

"He's a subcontractor specializing in reptile hunting. But he won't answer my calls anymore. Word on the street is that he wants to pitch a reality show about a dragon. We have to stop him. The last thing the world needs is another reality show."

Dreadrick prepared to unleash a barrage of curse words but held back. He was doomed and needed any help he could get. He absolutely had to get a dragon. He was so desperate, any dragon would do. As brilliant a mind as his could surely think of something.

And it did.

"Bonnard, I need you to find Bugg and get the dragon from him. I need it before tomorrow."

"I'm not sure I can—"

"And I have a backup plan as well. I need someone kidnapped. I don't care how much it costs."

MOLOCH THE MIGHTY, *Moloch the merciless, Moloch the mad as hell.*

It was twenty-four hours after he had found the note from

Agares, and Dreadrick had been lying in bed unable to sleep, wondering when Moloch would pay a visit.

When suddenly he was standing naked in a desert under a brutal sun. Before him was a tall hill, and then a giant figure ascended it from behind, silhouetted by the sun. It was a colossus. Two bull-like horns spread from the head of the silhouette that otherwise had the form of a giant human.

Dozens of glowing red eyes popped open on its head and chest.

Although Dreadrick was alone in this desert, he heard the murmur of hundreds of voices. They began to chant in an ancient, unknown language. The word "Moloch" was all he understood. Invisible hands pressed against his head, back, and arms, pushing him forward closer to the hill. Closer to Moloch. Two arms rose from the giant and beckoned to him.

"Wait," Dreadrick said. But his words were silent, as if he were dreaming.

Was he only dreaming? he wondered. That would be awesome!

The feel of the hands against his back were too real, though. The pain in his naked feet as they stumbled across the pebbly sand was too vivid.

And then, when Moloch opened his mouth, revealing the fire that burned inside the furnace of his torso, the smell of roasting flesh hit Dreadrick's nostrils.

No, this wasn't a dream, he realized. Was this the final act in the glorious saga of Morgan Dreadrick?

"Wait, I have a dragon for you!" he screamed through silent lips. "A dragon for you in my house."

And suddenly he was in his house, standing in the entrance of his two-story tall living room, with its gaudy furnishings and the statues he had looted from Iraq. There was also his newest prize: the cartoonish dragon mascot of the Orlando Magic. The eight-foot-tall, fuzzy green dragon stood in the middle of the room, wringing its gloved hands nervously. The thug Bonnard hired for the kidnapping job lurked in the corner of the room guarding the dragon.

"Where's Bonnard?" Dreadrick asked him.

"I don't know. He's not answering his phone."

"Mighty Moloch," Dreadrick said in a booming sorcerer's voice, his arms outstretched, trying to be as dramatic as possible despite the fact that he was still naked. "I present to you the most famous magic dragon, a sacrificial offering to your greatness."

He waited for a response from Moloch, though he wasn't sure in what form that would be.

"Sacrifice?" asked the flamboyant-sounding man in the dragon costume. "What exactly do you mean by that? And who is Moloch?"

"Shut up," the thug said.

"O mighty Moloch, please tell me that you accept my offering," Dreadrick intoned.

"Am I going to be killed?" the dragon asked, whining. He turned toward the thug. "You said you were taking me to a last-minute party for some rich guy who forgot it was his kid's birthday."

"Shut up, you weirdo," Dreadrick said. "O great Moloch, will you—"

Dreadrick was back in the desert, being pushed up the steep slope of the hill toward the angry god. His fake-dragon gambit had failed.

"O mighty one," Dreadrick said, "I have an offer for you. An offer you'll find irresistible. I have several hundred children for you that I'll gladly sacrifice. *Children.* Don't you love sacrificial children? I mean that's what you're famous for. How can you say no?"

Yet it was Dreadrick who couldn't scream "no!" loudly enough as he was pushed to the top of the mound and fell to his knees at the feet of the god. Now he could see the pitilessness in the many eyes that bore into him, judging him unworthy of immortality or even of life, judging his destiny to be nothing more than a tribute to an ancient god of greed and rapaciousness and constant hunger. The god that demanded the unthinkable.

Two hands, each bigger than Dreadrick himself, grasped him roughly, lifted him, and dropped him into the gaping mouth from which the fires of Hell raged.

And such was the untimely end of Morgan Dreadrick.

32

RESCUE ATTEMPT

Missy wasn't used to being awake in the daylight hours after all her time serving vampire patients. Fortunately, Matt was doing the driving as they headed south yet again. But this time it was to the Big Cypress Preserve on the northern part of Everglades National Park. Matt recommended they speak to a Miccosukee guide he had written a feature story about a couple of years ago. The man was known as the most knowledgeable guide around.

"His name is Billy Turner," Matt said. "His family has lived in the Everglades for generations. His passion for the land is infectious. When an oil company wanted to drill in Big Cypress, Billy was one of the leaders of the opposition. I'm also pretty sure he sabotaged some oil exploration equipment, but you didn't hear that from me."

"Bugg will be armed," Missy said. "Are you prepared for that? I'm warning you that my magick alone might not be enough to protect us."

"I understand. I'm sure Billy has weapons."

"Hopefully it won't come to that. I don't want to expose anyone else to danger. I just need to see how committed Billy is."

When she met Billy, her plans fell into place. He had a wide, olive-brown face with wrinkles around his eyes and a big grin. He removed his cowboy hat before shaking their hands. He invited them into an office at the Miccosukee Cultural Center at the edge of the reservation on U.S. Highway 41, Tamiami Trail.

"Why, you're the second person asking me about dragons," he said, sitting down behind a desk.

There was a rattlesnake hide hung on the wall behind him. Missy and Matt sat in chairs facing it.

"Really?" Missy asked. "Who was the other person?"

"Some investigator named Bonnard."

"We've met," Missy said.

Billy arched his eyebrows. "He wanted to pay me to help him find the dragon for some rich guy, but I turned him down."

"Because you don't believe in dragons?"

"Hell, yes, I believe in them. I've seen a couple myself over the years. The Everglades used to be teeming with them before humans moved in and began killing the land. But how do I know that your intentions are good?"

"I rescued the dragon when he was trapped in a sack that someone used to try to catch him. I nursed him back to health and got treatment for his broken wing. He's lived with me since then."

She sheepishly showed him a selfie of her and Ronnie in her garage.

"That photo is dangerous," Matt said. "Keep it secure."

"I know, but I couldn't resist."

"So you say that someone stole the dragon from you?" Billy asked.

"Yes," Missy said, recounting their encounter with Bugg, their escape, her victory over Bonnard, and then her discovery that Ronnie was missing from Squid Tower.

"Yeah, I've heard of that lowlife Bugg. He's a notorious gator poacher. But how can you be sure it was him who took the dragon?"

"Ronnie told me," Missy said. "Telepathically."

She expected Billy to break into laughter. Instead, he nodded his head solemnly.

"I've heard tales that they can talk, but I always thought it was just legend. And the telepathic part doesn't surprise me. Dragons have magick. That's how they control the gateway."

"You know of the gateway?" Missy asked with excitement.

"Yes. There is much about this land that non-native people will never know or understand. But this knowledge is part of my heritage. The gateway to other worlds is used by the dragons to protect themselves and avoid detection from humans. The gateway has always been here. The dragons learned how to control it long before humans existed."

Missy was thrilled to talk to someone who understood. Matt simply sat there silently with a wide-eyed expression.

"I've heard some of my people, generations ago, would cross back and forth through the gateway. But it is dangerous for humans to use it. Not a good idea."

"Yeah, I know," Missy said. "Not a good idea."

He looked at her with surprise.

"Will you help us?" she asked in a quiet voice.

"Of course, I will," Billy said, slapping the desk. "It's my duty. To help the dragons and put some hurt on that gator-poaching lowlife."

Missy opened a map app on her phone and showed Billy where she believed Bugg lived: a structure off a long dirt road that stretched south in a straight line from Tamiami Trail.

"I have a way to subdue him," Missy said, "but only temporarily."

"Martial arts?" Billy asked.

"A different kind of art. The thing is, we can't simply take the dragon and end up being chased by Bugg. He'll catch us eventually and take the dragon back."

"Can you get Ronnie out, and then call the sheriff on him?" Matt asked. "I bet there's evidence of his poaching all over the place, so he'll get arrested."

"Maybe, but we can't depend on that," Billy said. "You two come right to his front door and subdue him with her 'art.' Find the dragon and disable Bugg's truck, too. I'll come in from the back by airboat and take the dragon to safety so he won't know where it went. Text me when you're ready for me. I have to idle at least a quarter mile away because airboats are really loud, and he would hear me coming. But I'll drift and pole my way to his house. Afterwards, meet my boat at Everglades City, and I'll transfer the dragon to you."

Missy and Matt followed Billy who towed his airboat on a trailer behind a Ford F-250. They drove west along Tamiami Trail through the prairie wetlands where the occasional tiny tree islands broke the vast sweep of the river of grass. The sun was bright and the sky an unblemished blue. They crossed small bridges over ditches where egrets and herons stood like statues as they stalked fish next to alligators. It was beautiful and enchanting.

We're on our way, Ronnie, Missy spoke in her mind.

They came to the dirt road just past State Road 29 to Everglades City. As Matt's car stopped in a cloud of dust, the urgency and desperation of their situation came to the fore-front. Billy knocked on the window and both Matt and Missy jumped before Matt opened it.

"I'm going to launch the boat at the ramp up ahead," Billy said, "and head down the marsh that runs behind his cabin. You keep going and drive right up to his house like it's business as usual. You," he pointed at Matt, "go knock on the door and keep him occupied while she stays in the car, since Bugg will recognize her. After I drift up to his property, I'll approach from the rear."

Billy reached over Matt to hand Missy his business card.

"Text me when you've got him subdued or distracted. Or if you need me to bail you out. If I don't hear anything from you, I'm going in anyway."

Missy and Matt nodded. Matt's face was drained of blood.

"Good luck and be careful," Billy said.

They thanked him and watched him get into his truck and pull back onto the dirt road. He turned into a large lot next to an airboat-tour company where other airboats were launching and getting hauled out of the water.

"Is this Bugg guy going to blow my head off when I knock on his door?" Matt asked. He was sweating heavily despite the car's air conditioning.

"No," Missy said. "I'm about to cast a protection spell on you. Then I'll cast a binding spell to immobilize him. If I can, I'll even make him lose consciousness with a sleeping spell. If all goes well, you'll be able to walk right into his house and he'll be lying on the floor."

"Can you bind him without even seeing him?" Matt asked.

"If I have an accurate idea of where he is."

"So I can just walk inside the house with no problem?" He sounded doubtful.

"That's the idea. You don't trust my magick?"

"I have to admit it's taken me a while to come to terms with the fact you're a witch. But the truth is, I don't know if I trust anyone or anything with my life—not even a company of Marines let alone magick spells. What if Bugg isn't affected by the spell and stands there asking me why I'm there?"

"Make up a cover story. Like you're a photographer and want to take pictures on his property. Kill time while I try a different spell. If that doesn't work, just walk away. There's no reason for him to suspect your true intentions."

"And what if your spell works and the guy is unconscious, but Ronnie isn't in the house?"

"I'll be coming in behind you. We'll both look for him."

The dirt road went down the center of a narrow strip of land with creeks on either side. On their left were dense mangroves with occasional openings to open patches of water bending around tree islands. They passed a fisherman launching a johnboat into one of those openings.

"Will you look at that?" Matt said. "Someone ditched a car in the water over there. The middle of the Everglades shouldn't be treated like a junkyard."

In the shallows nearby the top half of a car rose above the surface. It was a silver Porsche with its windshield and driver's window shattered and full of bullet holes. It looked an awful lot like Bonnard's car. But Missy was no expert on Porsches.

Still, she had a bad feeling.

She focused her attention on casting the spells. It was much more difficult doing it in a moving car instead of inside a magick circle on the floor. But advancing in the mastery of magick required learning alternate ways of working spells. Her magick-on-the-go method involved carrying charms that each represented one of the five elements of earth, air, fire, water, and spirit.

She pricked her finger with a needle and pushed out a drop of blood, then chanted the invocation. The power filled her, humming and crackling like electricity. She directed it toward Matt. She watched him as he drove. A dark red aura became visible, indicating strength and the ability to survive. The protection spell was in place.

"I think I see the cabin ahead," Missy said. She tried to check her map app but there was no cellular service. "Remember, pull up right in front like we've got nothing to hide." She sank down in her seat below the window.

Matt parked beside the cabin. Missy raised her head to peek out her window. It was more like a garage or workshop shed than a cabin or house. It had a large barn-like door that looked like it hadn't been opened in years. There was a normal door without a porch and a very small closed window with dirty glass. The building had once been white but was now stained by mold and mildew and dead insects. A storage shed was to the side and rear of the house, near the edge of the marsh.

"Should I go to the door now, or wait?"

"The protection spell on you is working. I've cast the binding spell and I'm trying to attach it to Bugg. I don't think he's inside the house, but he is nearby."

"I'm going to knock on his door to flush him out," Matt said.

Missy focused on the binding spell, but things felt a little fuzzy.

Matt stepped out of the car.

And the windshield shattered as two gunshots rang out.

Matt dove to the ground behind the car. Missy couldn't help crying out as she sank lower in her seat. The shots sounded like they were coming from the direction of the storage shed. Her mind, jolted by panic, lost hold of the binding spell.

Another gunshot came from a closer location. A bullet punched into the hood.

She heard a whining sound. Then she realized it was coming from herself. She tried to calm down and resume the spell.

From nearby came the clicking of a magazine being replaced. She glanced up briefly and saw Bugg in the rearview mirror walking slowly toward the car, holding his pistol with two hands.

From the distance came a tremendous buzzing roar. It sounded like a prop airplane taxiing on a runway. Airboats use airplane engines, she remembered. Was that Billy coming to rescue them instead of sneaking up to the property?

Movement to her left caught her eye and she saw Matt low-crawling away from the car. He was either trying to divert the shooter's attention to protect her, or he was panicking and forgot he was protected by her spell. She decided to abandon the binding spell and cast a protection spell on herself before she was shot.

Another shot and a *thwack* of a bullet hitting a small tree on the other side of the road. Her hands were shaking. A protection spell had saved her from Bonnard's bullet. Was she absolutely certain it would work again if Bugg walked up to the car and emptied a magazine into it?

The airboat's engine was really loud now. It sounded like it had reached the shore behind the house.

More gunshots, but these came from behind the house. Bugg must have gone there to investigate the airboat. The boom of a shotgun joined Bugg's pistol fire. Billy was attacking. Missy ventured a quick look out the window and saw part of the airboat protruding behind the house, but she couldn't see Billy.

A bullet hit the doorframe right above her head and she dropped down to the floor.

Missy are you okay? It was Ronnie's voice.

No, we're not. He's going to kill us. Where are you?

In the shed. He moved me here because I was talking too much.

Ronnie, stay in the shed. I think he's going to kill Matt and me.

Mother! Ronnie screamed in her mind.

It was silent now, which concerned her. Bugg clearly wasn't dead, so why wasn't Billy shooting anymore? Was he all right?

A face popped up from below the passenger window beside her. She screamed.

"It's just me," Matt said. "Are you okay?"

"More or less. Where did you go?"

"I took a quick look inside the house. I didn't see Ronnie. I did see enough gator hides to put this guy in prison for a few years. And cases and cases of that whipped cream in a spray can. I think this nut job uses it to get high from the nitrous oxide."

Bugg appeared from behind the house, walking toward the car, reloading his gun.

"Get down!" she whispered.

At first it sounded like a helicopter overhead, a deep booming of air beaten by tremendous force. But it wasn't a helicopter's fast, machine-driven rotor blades. The beats were more irregular, more natural. The grass and low trees near the house shook in the wind.

Then she saw the shadow glide across the lawn and the roof of the house. And through the car's moonroof the enormous silvery belly scales came into view as it flew over her, followed by tucked-in rear legs, and then by the long, powerful, swinging tail and its arrowhead-shaped tip.

Ronnie's mother had arrived.

The dragon glided in a circle over the property, just above the height of the trees. She was gigantic yet elegant. The dark-brown body had patches of moss here and there which attested to her great age and many years in the Everglades. The horns angled back at the top of her head were long and shiny. Her wings were as large and mighty as the sails of a ship. Her muscular tail twitched behind her, snapping off the tops of trees.

The dragon saw Missy in the car, fixing her with a yellow reptilian eye. And if such a frightening creature could give a benevolent expression, this was it.

Ronnie's mother was simply magnificent. Missy could study her better now than when she had first been seen in the In-Between. The dragon radiated power and, yes, magick.

Bright light filled the car as the dragon belched flame and she smelled a strange, spicy scent. It was the smell of dragonfire.

Missy finally raised herself and looked out the window. Bugg ran by toward the house, his shirt and hair on fire. He paused to shoot at the dragon which was hovering only about thirty feet above the ground, her giant wings beating and rocking the car with their wind blasts. Her long neck arched to the fearsome head with yellow eyes fixed angrily on the evil human on the ground.

Missy didn't know if Ronnie's mother had been shot, but the dragon launched a thick stream of fire from her nostrils at Bugg as he retreated into the house. He shrieked as the flames enveloped him, yet managed to close the door behind him. The dragon hovered for a moment, watching the house.

Then she landed and walked on four legs to the shed. With one bite of her jaws, she wrenched the shed apart, the pieces of aluminum flying in all directions. Her body blocked Missy's view of what she was doing. But soon she was aloft again, with Ronnie grasped tenderly to her chest with her forelegs. As she slowly rose higher, she blasted the house with multiple jets of fire until it was a raging inferno.

She stopped shooting fire and banked, sailing to a higher altitude.

And then the sky broke apart.

Amid an explosion of thunder, the black line Missy had seen twice before stretched across the sky, a seam ripping open. A tornado descended from the black opening, extending downward like an arm reaching down for its quarry. The tornado tilted and moved toward Ronnie and his mother.

Extending downward as fast as a lightning bolt, the tornado plunged toward the dragon as she raced away across the sky. The tornado was going to hit her.

Until the adult dragon deftly changed direction, wings beating furiously, and the twister shot past her, hitting the nearby marsh. Water and fragments of plants flew in the air and rained upon Bugg's property like the contents of a blender with its cover removed.

The tornado switched directions and followed Ronnie's mother like an arm probing blindly.

"I have a feeling the gateway is nearby," Missy said to Matt, "but I don't know if she can make it."

The tornado just missed the dragons again. Ronnie's mother nearly got sucked into the vortex. She careened away from the funnel cloud, flapping her wings and swinging downward. She landed on a small island on the marsh, perhaps to rest or adjust her grip on Ronnie.

The tornado turned and sped toward her.

"Do you know a spell that can help?" Matt asked.

"Maybe. Give me some silence so I can concentrate."

She thought back to science class and tried to remember all she could about tornadoes. Something about warm, moist air hitting colder air, then thunderstorms, then the warm air pushing up through the cold air. . .

Of course, this tornado was supernatural in its origins. So the idea that popped in her head of mimicking the way that tornadoes dissipate might not work. Especially since she had only tried this spell before on a much smaller scale. In her house, to be honest, when her central air broke during a heat wave. But it was worth a try.

She grasped the power charm in her pocket and gathered all the earth-energy she could summon from the land and water around her. Then she combined it with the powers that resided deep within her that were her birthright from her parents.

She whispered the incantation and felt the air temperature drop drastically. A bitter-cold wind picked up from the west, blowing the smoke from the burning house away from them, almost extinguishing the raging fire.

She directed the zephyr toward the tornado. And soon the twister stumbled in its rotation as the cold air disrupted the unstable mix of weather conditions that gave it its power.

The twister touched down in the water again, creating a waterspout that quickly dissipated.

The tornado was gone. She released the zephyr from her service. Ronnie's mother took flight again.

And slammed into an invisible wall. Sluggishly flapping her wings, she descended to the island once more.

Was she okay? Missy worried.

That's when the day turned into night as heavy darkness cloaked the landscape.

And several pairs of glowing red eyes moved toward the dragons. The eyes were at least fifty feet in the air, a swarm of malevolent fireflies.

She gasped. It was Moloch.

"What is that?" Matt asked in a stunned voice.

Ronnie, Missy cried to him telepathically. *Tell your mother to connect with me. We need to combine our powers.*

Okay, his voice said in her head.

Immediately, she felt the presence of someone else inside her mind. It was an even closer connection than hearing the words of telepathic speech. It was closer, even, than the intuitive mental bond of two people who have been in love for years.

She felt greater than herself.

She also carried the weight of history and the wisdom of centuries. Her senses were heightened, and she smelled every particle of carbon from every material burning in the fire. Beneath that she smelled the nutrient-rich Everglades muck and its abundant vegetable life, the pollens and juices and spores. She smelled the fear of nearby mammals and the excrement of birds. The scent of the fish in the marshes and the invertebrates digging in the sand.

She smelled the leathery smell of her reptilian scales and felt the scars from battles decades ago. She could see, better than her human eyes, the outline of Moloch marching across the dirt road toward her.

She felt the coolness of the water and the soft, yielding sand as the dragon burrowed into the bottom of the marsh with her dragon child, hiding in the manner her species had done in the Everglades for millennia.

And she knew that Moloch must be stopped. She understood that perhaps gods couldn't be permanently killed, but nevertheless could have their existence terminated so they were no longer anything more than references in history books and ancient religious texts.

How do we combine Missy's human magick with a dragon's instinctive powers? the two consciousness both wondered.

For Moloch to direct attacks against us, he must have some degree of existence in the material realm, Ronnie's mother said. *The more he transforms himself into matter, the more he is vulnerable to the laws of physics.*

Moloch's footsteps were like tiny earthquakes as he plodded toward the spot where the dragons were burying themselves beneath the shallow water.

Missy had an idea for the kind of spell she needed, but she didn't have a grimoire with instructions on how to cast it, if such a spell even existed. She would have to conjure it through instinct and intuition.

The darkness created by Moloch had diminished slightly, or perhaps Missy's eyes had compensated for it. The giant god's silhouette was visible beyond the burning house, wading through the marsh. Thunderous splashes and sucking sounds accompanied his footsteps.

The dragons' fear ran through her. The ancient god was almost upon them. She felt them buried in the mud and sand, the mother's head protruding enough to breech the surface of the water in order to breathe. Her child was in temporary hibernation to conserve oxygen.

The earth beneath the marsh shook from the weight of a giant. Moloch was upon them now. He leaned over, his bull's head close to the surface of the water. His bovine nostrils widened as he sniffed, his clusters of red eyes roving the marsh, looking for his victims.

He snorted like a bull as he reached with his human-like arm and claw-like hand.

Missy was at least a hundred yards away, but the blasts of dragonfire were so powerful they nearly blinded her. The heat of them was greater even than the nearby house fire.

Moloch bellowed with pain and jerked backwards.

More jets of fire shot from the dragon's head protruding from the water. The giant god stumbled backwards away from the source of its pain.

He truly is of material substance now, Missy thought, and that's why the fire is harming him.

She continued trying to formulate a spell to harm Moloch more than the dragonfire could. She tried to consolidate the dragon's magick with her own. Energy was energy and power was power, but still the dragon's felt different than hers. It ebbed and flowed while it fought the ancient god.

She didn't have the feeling of unity with the dragon that she had before. There was too much fear as the mother fought to save herself and her child.

Moloch roared in pain as fire shot from the surface of the water and wrapped around his legs, rising to engulf his torso and head.

He stumbled backwards, splashing through the marsh, swatting at himself to smother the fire. He retreated further and sat down in the water with a seismic impact. He splashed himself with water and doused the flames.

Now is the time to strike, Missy thought. But she couldn't summon the power sufficient for her spell.

Please help me, she implored Ronnie's mother. *Share your power with me so we can destroy him.*

One hundred yards away, the colossus sat in the marsh, his dark form unmoving.

Until its clusters of red eyes darted in Missy's direction.

Uh-oh, she thought.

The god slowly returned to his feet. And began plodding toward her.

He must have sensed my psychic connection with the dragon, she thought. And he wants to get rid of me.

The heavy footfalls splashed through the marsh. One foot stomped on a small island, crushing it. His many red eyes were focused on Missy. The lips drew back on his bull muzzle in a grimace like a smile.

"Run!" she said to Matt as she drew closer to the burning house, hoping its flames would be a barrier.

The giant was close now, towering above the spit of land. Her hands shook with her fear.

The blast of a shotgun roared behind the house, followed by another. At least Billy was still alive, she thought, but not for long if Moloch attacked him.

Unable to cast the spell she wanted, she frantically tried to invoke a binding spell to stop the giant. She whispered the words and focused her power. A net appeared that only she could see, suspended in the air in front of the giant at the edge of the marsh behind the house. It was taller and wider than the giant, taut strands of magick as strong as steel. She pumped more power into it.

Moloch stumbled into the barrier and stopped. He bellowed in anger. The tension in the strands of magick as the god strained against them gave Missy an ache in the back of her skull.

The colossus glared down at her with his multiple insect eyes, sizing her up. She didn't know what he was capable of in material form or in the spiritual realm. And she didn't want to find out. She wanted to hop in the car and get out of there, but knew she couldn't leave the dragons to face this monster alone.

She returned her attention to creating the spell to defeat Moloch. The problem was, she needed some mental power to maintain the binding spell. It wasn't a set-it-and-forget-it kind of spell.

At last, she felt the waves of the mother dragon's magick pouring into her.

She retreated from her position near the house and walked up the road a short distance. She couldn't concentrate with an ancient god only a stone's throw away, straining against a magical net in order to kill her. She closed her eyes, calmed herself, and focused her thoughts. She went into a Zen-like state. Soon, the framework of the new spell was coming together.

"You think you're so smart, pretty lady?"

She opened her eyes. Bugg stood in front of her, pointing a scorched handgun at her. He was naked, his clothes having been burned away along with his hair. All his hair, from his body and head. But he didn't appear to have any serious burns on his pasty white, flabby skin.

"Oh my," she said. "How did you survive the fire?"

"My cans of Weddy Whip exploded, and the whipped cream put out enough of the flames long enough to let me escape."

She jumped at the release of tension as the binding spell broke due to her distraction.

"You were lucky," she said. "But now you have really bad timing."

"Funny. You're the one whose time has just run out," said Bugg as he aimed the pistol.

"You too. We're both about to be killed by an ancient god. A really angry one."

"Ha-ha. You can't fool me."

He said this a half-second before a giant claw came from above and grabbed him.

Screaming hysterically, he struggled to escape the giant claw. He looked like Fay Wray being picked up by King Kong. Except Moloch had a very different intention than the giant ape.

Bugg's screams were cut off abruptly as he went into the ancient god's mouth.

Moloch chewed carefully before swallowing.

Missy took off running. She had to follow the dirt road because there was very little other solid ground on the narrow spit of land. The earth shook as the giant pursued her. She had no illusions that she could escape Moloch this way, but she hoped to gain time while she tried to complete the new spell.

If only she could do it while running and without collapsing in a pile of quivering fear for her life.

Suddenly, on top of her panic, she felt an existential fear. It was the same feeling she'd had near the gateway. She turned her head. Moloch lumbered down the road close behind her. But a transparent, shimmering wall was moving across the road into his path.

Was Ronnie's mother trying to help her by moving the gateway?

Moloch saw the gateway at the last minute and tried to stop. But a giant of his size and weight could not stop on a dime. He hit the shimmering wall and disappeared.

Missy stopped running and tried to catch her breath. The gateway remained in the road shimmering. She knew there was a good chance Moloch might return so she resumed assembling the complex latticework that would comprise the spell to defeat him once and for all.

The gateway darkened and the shimmering increased. The view through it of the road behind her faded as the gateway turned an opaque green.

It seemed to tear open.

And a giant claw darted out and grabbed her, pulling her through the opening.

The world disappeared.

33

MISSY VS. MOLOCH

Missy landed face-first in sand. She pushed herself to her feet, wiped the sand from her face and spit the grains from her mouth. The sand and the air were burning hot. She was on a flat landscape that appeared to be the top of a mesa about 150 yards long and half that distance wide. Its surface was broken up by boulders and low ridges of rock. Far below the mesa was a brown, desert-like countryside. All was bathed in a harsh, white light. The sky was white and there was no orb of a sun.

She assumed she was in the In-Between, but wasn't positive. And she was definitely here physically, as in her visit with Ronnie. It wasn't an astral visit like when she had asked the souls about Schwartz.

Which was a problem. Because Moloch was here with her.

The giant's head appeared above the rim of the mesa. Back in her world, he always brought night-like darkness with him. Here, he was bathed in the white light and she saw him more clearly than ever before.

Ugliness has nothing to do with evil, but evil was manifest in Moloch's hideous visage. The black fur of his bull head was blotchy and discolored, crisscrossed with scars and gouges caused by long-ago violence. His flaring nostrils were cracked and bloody. His two long horns were notched and stained. A battered tongue hung from the side of his mouth.

But the most awful features were his eyes. The bull's eyeballs were missing, leaving only empty sockets. Instead, it saw with the clusters of tiny, red, glowing eyes that appeared randomly all over its face and chest like measles. They rolled about in all directions until all thirty to forty of them focused on her.

I want the young dragon.

The voice invading her head spoke in a guttural, ancient language she had never heard before, but somehow, she understood it.

"I can't help you," she said aloud.

I can command a demon to possess you and make you obey my orders.

"I'd rather die."

A low, loud rumble came from the giant's throat, echoing in the canyon below. He opened his mouth. His bovine teeth were yellow and worn, but each was about as tall as she was.

Then you will die. And it will be slow and painful. My power on Earth is not what it once was when hundreds of thousands of humans worshipped me and sacrificed their children at my altar to beseech my favors. But here I am stronger. Here I am nearer to Hell where I reign with the other forgotten gods. I will give you a taste of the pain that witches endured before dying at the hands of humans. And then I will torture you in ways that humans have never imagined.

A powerful wind knocked her backwards onto the ground, a sharp rock slicing her scalp. The sensation of burning swept through her entire body as if it had caught on fire yet burned without flames. Moloch was right: His supernatural powers were greater here in the In-Between.

She screamed from the searing pain—the mind-destroying agony of fire. She rolled over and over upon the ground, trying to put out the flames that were not real. The searing pain was overwhelming, maddening. And the hopelessness of her situation was breaking her down. She wasn't home or even on the same plane of existence as home. She was alone.

And she was lost.

Dragons, please help me.

Would Ronnie and his mother hear her when she was in the In-Between?

After I kill you, I will return to the Everglades and kill the young dragon, the guttural voice echoed in her head. *Your death will be in vain.*

Tears flowed from her eyes as she writhed upon the sand and rocks.

"Please stop!" she screamed.

And I will kill your human friends as well.

"No, leave them alone. There's no reason to kill them."

The reason is that you defy me. If you want them to live, if you want to spare your own life, you must obey me.

She wanted to conjure some magick to fight back against Moloch, or at least to relieve her pain. But she couldn't concentrate enough to cast even the easiest spell. The pain was too much.

"Why do you need me to help you?" she managed to ask. "You can kill the dragon yourself."

Indeed I can. But I prefer the dragon be given to me as a sacrifice. Blood sacrifice is what made me strong when I was a god upon the earth. The act of betrayal in the bringing of a victim you care for to slaughter gives me power over my worshippers. And this particular dragon has deep veins of power that will flow to me.

"I can't—"

Her pain suddenly increased. A lot. She let out a keening cry as she twisted in the sand. She wanted to die. Fast. Anything to end the burning. If she had been engulfed in real flames, she would have been dead by now, free of all suffering.

But this agony could go on forever. She sobbed, not caring about the sand in her mouth and eyes and how pitiful she had become.

"I'll do it," she gasped. "Stop my pain now and I'll do it. I'll call the dragon here to you."

You must personally give the young dragon to me to kill.

"I will," she said.

And the pain was gone.

MATT WAS FLABBERGASTED. He had just seen a giant monster emerge from a dark cloud and swallow Bugg whole. It chased Missy down the dirt road. Then the monster simply disappeared. Matt had been convincing himself that the entire thing was a figment of his imagination, a flashback of some sort from illegal substances he consumed back in college.

He was close to having logic prevail and convince himself that he had not seen what he saw, when out of nowhere, a giant claw appeared in the spot where the giant had disappeared. And it plucked Missy from the ground before they both vanished.

Maybe he was simply going insane. Yeah, that would explain it.

The heat from the raging fire was intense enough to interrupt his mental-health evaluation. He worried the car would catch fire. He started it and drove it north along the dirt road out of harm's way, but close enough for easy access. He was afraid Billy would need to be taken to medical care.

Matt returned to the property. Behind it, Billy's airboat was beached on a grassy spot. Closer to the house, two legs jutted out from behind a tree.

"Billy? You okay?" he called.

"I've been better."

Matt came to him through clouds of smoke. Billy sat leaning against the tree, his shotgun held against his chest with its stock resting on the ground. His left leg was drenched in blood.

"I can't drive an airboat," Matt said, "so we'll have to leave it here while I take you to a hospital. Or at least to somewhere I can get a cell signal to call 911."

"Where's Miss Mindle?" Billy asked in a voice tight with pain.

"Um, Missy disappeared. I guess it was through the gateway you guys were talking about. Did you see the giant?"

"I saw something huge, but it was inside dark clouds. Was it supernatural?"

"I guess. And it took Missy. I don't know how to help her."

"There's no way to help. We don't know how to find the gateway."

Matt removed the lace of one of his sneakers and used it as a tourniquet on Billy's upper thigh. The wound was in the front of his lower thigh with an expansive exit wound in the rear where his jeans were torn to shreds. He supported the man as he limped to the car and helped him into the front seat.

"Let's go to the boat ramp area where a helicopter can land," Billy said. "I think I need to go to a trauma center, not just any hospital. Use my phone to call 911. My carrier is the only one that works out here."

Matt made the call and was assured a Life Flight chopper would be dispatched. As soon as he hung up, the frame of Bugg's house collapsed, sending ash and embers across the yard. The intense heat of the dragonfire had obliterated everything aside from the concrete slab.

"Did Bugg make it out of the house?" Billy asked.

"Actually he did."

"Really? So where did he go?"

"He went on a food run."

Before he could explain to a perplexed Billy, loud splashing came from the marsh behind the burning house. The adult dragon emerged from the water and took flight. She circled over the marsh, sticking close to the ground, landing not far away from them. She set Ronnie on the ground and he scampered to the car.

Matt rolled down his window.

"Missy is calling for us to help her," Ronnie said. "She's in the In-Between and Moloch has her. We have to save her."

Matt's stomach sank. Missy's situation was as bad as he feared.

"Godspeed, little guy," he said to Ronnie.

"Don't call me 'little,' dogface."

Ronnie returned to his mother. She picked him up and sprang into the air. The car rocked back and forth from the blasts of wind displaced from her flapping wings. The adult dragon again flew low to the ground, probably to avoid detection from radar or human eyes.

Then she disappeared.

34

ANTI-MOLOCH MATTER

M issy sat, hugging her legs to her chest. Every few moments she shook uncontrollably. She was no longer suffering the pain of being burned alive and her body was unhurt. But she suffered from the psychological trauma. She hoped it wouldn't last.

Moloch's face was no longer above the rim of the mesa. She got to her feet and walked unsteadily toward the edge. The mesa was about five stories above the surrounding countryside. There was no sign of Moloch.

Off in the distance, a small part of the featureless white sky began to shimmer. She caught her breath.

A dragon appeared, flying toward her.

As it came closer, it looked familiar. It was Ronnie's mother. She reached the mesa and circled it as she descended, landing nearby. Her yellow eyes fixed upon Missy's.

"We must hurry," she spoke aloud. It was the first time Missy had heard her voice. It was high-pitched and full of hissing and, like Ronnie, she had a bit of a Southern accent.

"Is Ronnie safe?"

"Yes, I left him in a good hiding spot in another realm of the In-Between. We must resume our work together now. Moloch has more power here than he did on earth."

"I know. And, unfortunately, I have less," Missy said. "I can't access the power in the earth here."

Since she had room to do so, unlike the last time she worked on the spell, she drew a pentagram surrounded by a magick circle in the sand. Even without the earth power, the circle would amplify her own. She knelt inside of it, grasped the charms in her pocket, and began an incantation to open her mind and spirit. She summoned the power deep inside her to rise up.

Ronnie's mother settled down into a crouch and folded her wings on her back, tucking her head beneath one of them like a sleeping bird. Immediately, Missy felt the dragon's mind reaching out to hers. Missy accepted it and soon she felt as if she were inside the dragon's head, experiencing her senses and emotions.

There was fear and anxiety in the dragon, just like she felt. Yet there was also strong determination. And beneath it all, Missy felt the mother's love for Ronnie and the savage will to protect him at all costs. The dragon's power slowly seeped into Missy and commingled with hers.

Missy began to reassemble the spell she had worked on before. It was a delicate and complex framework of many layers and levels. She wove it to be flexible yet exceptionally strong. And it needed every bit of power she had, as well as the dragon's.

When Moloch comes, do not be distracted, the dragon telepathically said. *You will be protected.*

Missy didn't answer. She continued working. She had never

before attempted to create a spell as powerful as this. The most fundamental laws of atomic energy were involved, manipulated by magick. She felt excitement as her work progressed, but was anxious about completing it and making it work.

And she was terrified of the damage it could cause if it went wrong.

Because she was conjuring the equivalent of antimatter.

Her theory was that Moloch existed in material form because of his evil supernatural power. He essentially created matter out of black magic. If, using her white magick, she could create the opposite of the material that formed him, her creation and his would destroy each other, just as antiparticles destroy their equivalent particles, such as antiprotons negating protons.

That's how she would explain it to someone like Matt. A witch might say creating something "anti" sounds evil. Missy would explain, on the contrary, her spell was "anti-evil." It would counteract the evil that created the matter that was stomping around, eating Bugg, and trying to kill a dragon prodigy. Not to mention torturing her.

And speak of the devilish god, the ground began shaking rhythmically. The thunder of massive impacts grew louder and louder.

Moloch was back. He snorted, deep and wet. It echoed throughout the canyon around the mesa.

Have you brought the young dragon? the guttural voice said in her mind.

Missy chanted the words she had chosen to craft the finishing touches on the spell.

Ignore him, Ronnie's mother said, her words pushing Moloch's from her mind.

The giant's head appeared above the rim of the mesa. He was pissed off, to put it lightly.

I don't see the young dragon. Have you disobeyed me?

His multitude of tiny red eyes darted in all directions. He bellowed like an angry bull, hurting her ears.

His eyes suddenly looked upward.

It sounded like dozens of axes chopping trees, but, in fact, it was the flapping of twelve pairs of dragon wings high in the white sky. A formation of adult dragons one after another, in a long winding line, descended toward the mesa.

They will protect us while we work, Ronnie's mother said.

The sand around Missy and her ally rose in small whirl-winds as the air swirled from the wings beating overhead. The dragons were roughly the size of Ronnie's mother, some larger but most of them smaller. The amounts of moss and discolorations on their brownish-green hides indicated the older ones. Missy was filled with awe at the magnificent sight, but forced herself to focus on her task.

Just before Moloch reached the mesa, the dragons attacked. Twelve jets of fire hit him from every angle. He covered his face with his clawed hands and bellowed, staggering backwards.

The smell of burned flesh filled the air. But it was not true, organic flesh. It had been the corrupt creation of black magic.

Missy readied the spell to destroy it. Since, in the In-Between she couldn't draw upon the power in the earth, she added an extra boost: the pocket of energy she had stored inside her ever since her consciousness had floated above the Krome Service Processing Center. It was the distillation of human spirit—the concentrated negative energy of the despairing men inside the facility.

Their negative energy would be turned into a positive force

as it was added to the spell she had created. Now it was time for the last, critical ingredient.

"Release the rest of your power to me now," Missy said aloud to Ronnie's mother.

Missy shuddered. Her mind felt like it was exploding. Intense blue light filled her vision and buzzing engulfed her hearing. The scent of an electrical fire overcame the stench of burning flesh. Her body rose a few inches from the ground. Her breathing and her heartbeat both stopped.

She hung suspended in silence, darkness, nothingness.

Then she landed on the sand again. Her vision returned and she heard again the beating of leathery wings and the grunts of pain coming from Moloch. The dragons flew in a circle above the giant, diving down to shoot fire at him. He swatted at them as if he were surrounded by a cloud of mosquitoes.

Missy felt utterly empty, exhausted, and numb. She was too spent to move. Ronnie's mother remained crouched nearby, her head still tucked under a wing.

A couple hundred yards away, Moloch swiped at a dragon that had flown too close to him. One claw sliced the dragon's side, drawing blood, but the creature managed to stay aloft and escaped to a safer distance.

And then the apparition rose from the top of the mesa.

Missy could describe it only as a white shadow.

It was over fifty feet tall, like Moloch, and it had the exact same shape as his. She had difficulty seeing the white shadow against the white sky, but it did stand out when it had the brownish landscape as a backdrop. As far as she could tell, it was meant to be Moloch's shadow, except it was white instead of black. It was light instead of the absence of light. It was the twin of Moloch, except that it was good instead of evil.

The white shadow walked across the mesa without making a sound. There were no impacts from its footsteps. It jumped off the mesa, landing in front of Moloch who had retreated a short distance while the dragons attacked him. The dragons, having noticed the shadow, flew away, landing on a low hill in the distance where they watched what was about to occur.

The white shadow of Moloch approached its in-the-flesh counterpart. From her vantage atop the mesa, Missy could see the shadow easily as it stood out from countryside behind it. Moloch saw it too. He bellowed in rage and approached it to attack. He obviously didn't understand what the shadow was and its danger to him.

The white shadow matched every movement Moloch made, as a true shadow would. When Moloch attempted to slash the shadow with the claws of his right hand, the shadow mirrored the action. Moloch's arm froze just as it was about to connect with the shadow's arm. It was as if a strong pane of glass separated them.

Moloch tried with his left arm. The white shadow mimicked the movement and Moloch's arm was blocked. The ancient god roared with frustration and lunged at his shadow with both arms wide for tackling. Again, he was blocked.

He stepped back and surveyed his shadow. Missy sensed the presence of black magic beginning to emanate from the god. The shadow needed to perform its duty quickly before Moloch managed to cause problems, but Missy no longer had any control over the entity she had conjured.

She didn't need to worry. The white shadow flew at Moloch, wrapping its arms and legs around the ancient god.

A ball of white fire appeared in the center of the two of them. It was so bright Missy had to avert her eyes.

Then came the explosion. It was like a nuclear bomb. First there was the blinding light eclipsing the landscape, then the short but eardrum-damaging crack, and then the blast of wind and sand bowling Missy over onto her side. She rolled so that her back faced the scourging sand.

When the last fragment of debris landed and all was quiet, Missy stood and surveyed the scene. There was no smoke. The countryside was just as bright as it had been under the light of the sunless sky. Where Moloch had stood was a blackened crater, almost as large as the mesa itself. A wide fissure gaped at the bottom of the crater.

Moloch was gone.

Missy had the strangest feeling of being watched. Not by Moloch or any antagonistic enemy. But by someone who knew her. She sensed warmth, approval, and pride. It was as if the watcher had waited years for Missy to have achieved what she did today.

Her imagination made the leap that it was one of her birth parents looking down at her from Heaven.

Don't be too proud, she thought, this evil monster could come crawling back out of that crater any minute now, with my luck.

As if reading Missy's mind, Ronnie's mother spoke out loud.

"His manifestation in the material world was completely destroyed," the dragon said. "Moloch is back in Hell, existing in the weakened state of a god that has been forgotten."

"Is he still a threat?" Missy asked.

"Not for now. He would be too weak to return to the material world for quite some time. Perhaps someday he will regain enough power to come here to the In-Between, but he would be little more than an apparition. We dragons can deal with him here if he ever appears. He wouldn't be able to return to earth on his own probably for centuries."

"What do you mean, 'on his own'?"

"I can't promise that a misguided practitioner of the black arts won't try to summon him. But I wouldn't worry now about any threat from Moloch."

"Good riddance," Missy said.

The two were silent, watching the dragons reappear from behind a hill where they had taken cover. They flew over the mesa, then passed into a shimmering section of sky, and disappeared.

"Did they go to the Everglades?" Missy asked.

"To another part of the In-Between we call our own. But I will send you back to earth, to the last place you were before coming here."

"Um, let's make sure that Matt and the car are still there. I don't want to be stranded in the Everglades. I don't have wings for flying."

Ronnie's mother made a sound like a laugh.

"I never asked you your name," Missy said. "Ronnie told you mine, but he never told me yours."

She expected to hear a majestic name appropriate to the dragon's more than 120 years of life, something cool like Meraxes or Stormfyre.

Instead, the dragon replied, "Girl Dragon."

"I meant your *name*," Missy said.

"The human who raised me named me Girl Dragon. And he didn't even know I was female without my telling him so."

"He wasn't very poetic, was he?"

"He was a pineapple farmer. He didn't have much use for poetry. And I should know. Dragons don't have a writing system, but we've always had an oral tradition of poetry. Usually the heroic kind, with dragons slaying evil knights."

"I'd love to see you again," Missy said. "And hear a poem or two."

GIRL DRAGON CAUSED the gateway to appear on the mesa (Missy had no idea how dragons were able to do that). Missy said goodbye and asked her to give her farewell to Ronnie. Sad but anxious to get her life back to normal, she stepped through the gateway. . .

. . . and stumbled upon the dirt parking area of a boat ramp in the Everglades, the one nearest Bugg's cabin. No one noticed her awkward arrival because all eyes were on the helicopter taking off. It was a medical-transport aircraft and Missy's heart leaped to her throat wondering if it carried Matt or Billy.

Matt tapped her on the shoulder. He looked unharmed.

"Was that Billy?" she asked.

"Yeah. He got shot in the leg. The medical crew thinks he'll make it, though. So do you mind telling me where you disappeared to? You've been gone for like forty-five minutes!"

"I was in the In-Between for several hours, but I guess time moves differently there. I went when Moloch grabbed me and pulled me through the gateway."

"Ronnie told me you called for him and his mother to help," Matt said. "How?"

"You know that telepathic thing I have with them? Well, I asked Ronnie's mother for help and told her to bring Ronnie to a safe place first. I needed to buy time and stop Moloch from torturing me. He wanted me to lure Ronnie to him to be sacrificed, which I would never do, of course. And I needed his mother with me so I could add her power to mine and create a spell strong enough to stop Moloch. Which it did."

"Nothing you just said makes any sense to me. But what is this about being tortured?"

"I'll explain. I just can't talk about it now," Missy sad. "Let's drive to the hospital where they took Billy and wait for him to get out of surgery. And their gift shop better have some junk food. I need a sugar high big time."

35

PRETTY PROSE

To Agnes, things appeared back to normal at Squid Tower. Schwartz's Lexus was once again parked illegally in the handicapped space and he had already emailed two complaints to the HOA about landscape maintenance issues. Agnes couldn't help but wonder if getting him back was such a good idea.

One difference at Squid Tower was that Missy couldn't show up tonight to teach her creative-writing workshop. She said she was in Ft. Myers with a friend who was in the hospital. So Agnes agreed to stand in as the moderator. She greeted the group that was already sitting in chairs arranged in a circle in the community room.

"Hello, everyone. I'm here in place of Missy who has a friend with a medical emergency."

The class seemed a little apprehensive at first. No one wanted to be the first to read their work out loud.

"Are you folks always this shy?" Agnes asked.

"Well, this is your first time here, "Marjorie said. "It's not easy to share your inner thoughts and emotions with your neighbors. It took us a while to get used to reading in front of each other. And with Missy, too."

"Partly because she's not a vampire," Sol said.

"I understand," Agnes said. "And I won't judge you. So who wants to begin?"

Silence. A rustling of papers.

"What about you, Bill? You don't seem like the shy type."

"Um, I'm not sure I feel comfortable right now."

"Is it because I'm the president of the HOA?" Agnes asked.

"No," Bill said. "To be frank, it's because you were the wife of a Visigoth general and you look like you'd rather thrust a spear into a Roman's stomach than listen to pretty prose."

"Okay, okay, I'll go," Gladys said.

Sol groaned.

"That's not polite, Sol," Agnes said.

"Sorry, but I get embarrassed when I listen to vampire porn."

"It's not porn!" Gladys said with indignation. "I write passionate romance. I'll have you know that romance is the best-selling category of fiction. I could get rich writing it."

"Not the way you write," Sol muttered under his breath, but everyone heard him.

"Why don't you proceed, Gladys," Agnes said.

Gladys cleared her throat. "My story is called 'Hot-Blooded.'"

Sol groaned.

"Lady Amaranth awoke at dusk in her castle chambers," Gladys read, "to the throbbing hum of the shrubbery being trimmed in the grounds below her window."

"Point of fact," Bill interrupted, "motorized trimmers weren't invented until the Twentieth Century."

"She just wanted to work 'throbbing' in there somehow," Sol said.

"Gentlemen, stop being rude," Agnes said.

Her tone of voice shut them up and turned their faces a shade paler than they already were.

"Lady Amaranth peered out of her window and looked down at the landscaper," Gladys continued, "a hunk of a man without a shirt whose pectoral muscles quivered from his effort. His abs were a six-pack of steel beneath smooth skin shiny with sweat."

Sol covered his eyes and shook his head.

"'Who could this young peasant be?' Lady Amaranth wondered. 'I've never seen him before. Wouldn't it be lovely to sink my fangs into his brawny neck?' Then she watched, fascinated, as the young hunk picked up a shovel, gripped its long shaft, and plunged it over and over into the soft, yielding earth. Again and again he thrust the tool, panting with his exertion."

"Oh, I'm sorry, I just received an important text," Agnes lied. "I need to step out to handle some HOA business. Please continue without me."

"Can I go with you?" Sol asked her.

AGNES LEFT the workshop even more impressed with Missy. Managing this class on a weekly basic appeared to be more difficult than summoning an army of iguanas. Also, Agnes had heard a rumor that Missy had recently battled an ancient god. She was a pretty tough cookie for a mortal human.

Agnes strolled outside to the swimming pool deck. Her vampire hearing picked up the voices of Oleg and Schwartz. Not wanting to disturb them, she hung back.

"Thailand?" Oleg asked Schwartz incredulously. "Haven't you learned your lesson?"

"Yeah," Schwarz said on the pool lounger next to Oleg's. The two were soaking in the moonlight amid the balmy ocean breezes. "But the girls there are legendary."

"Now that you know how vulnerable we freaks are when we cross borders, you would actually suggest that?"

"Okay. Never mind."

"We could have been staked," Oleg said. "And look what happened to you?"

"It was all because of the werewolf blood. I made a stupid mistake."

"Doesn't mean they can't find out what we are in other ways. I'm never leaving this country again. Or, if I do, I'll only fly in a private jet. Getting through Customs is a breeze that way."

"Private jets are too expensive," Schwartz said.

"To Thailand, yes. To the Dominican Republic it wouldn't have been too bad. We shouldn't have been so cheap. Look at what happened."

"If we get a bunch of other vampires to share the cost, maybe I'll reconsider."

"I don't think there are a 'bunch' of other vampires who would go," Oleg said. "I don't think there are more than a handful in Squid Tower who can make the elevator rise to the top floor, if you know what I mean."

"Hence the werewolf blood," Schwartz said.

Oleg uttered an oath in Russian. "Subject closed," he stated.

The two were silent for a while so Agnes listened to the rumbling of the surf nearby. The drunken werewolves at Seaweed Manor had finally turned off their music so it was nice and quiet.

"Doesn't it feel great to be home again?" Oleg asked.

"Yeah, until I found someone parking in my spot."

"It's not your spot. It's a handicapped spot."

"I've got bad knees," Schwartz said. "I tried to get the car towed but the HOA doesn't allow non-vampire towing services in here."

"Of course. You don't want humans poking around here during the day when we're asleep, do you?"

"In New York, there was a towing service run by vampires for vampires."

"There you go again," Oleg said. "Disparaging Florida. You've been doing that for a hundred years ever since you moved here. Can't you simply enjoy what you have? Just a few days ago you were chained up in a shipping container. You would have been staked if we hadn't rescued you."

"Not if I made that guy a vampire. I should have done it. Who cares if he couldn't adapt and ended up dying?"

"We've already discussed that. It's against the vampire moral code to turn evil people into vampires. We don't want to exist in a world with monsters like that."

"Whatever," Schwartz said. "This pool needs cleaning. Things are really going downhill in this place. Budget cuts. Always budget cuts."

"And if they raised the HOA fees to cover more cleaning you'd go ballistic. Leonard, why can't you stop being Schwartz and just enjoy eternal life?"

"I guess I can't help being Schwartz. It's who I am."

They were silent for a while.

"I hear they have really sweet *chicas* in Cancun," Schwartz said.

"No. I'm not leaving home for a long time."

"It's a super-short flight. C'mon, Oleg. Your old riding crop still has some snap to it, huh?"

"I'll think about it, Schwartz. But not tonight."

Agnes contemplated the absurdity of the two old vampires. They'd had hundreds of years upon the earth to gather wisdom and an eternity ahead of them in which to use it. Yet here they were, trying to be adolescent mortals again.

They weren't just undead, she thought. They were unbearable.

36

EMPTY NESTER

A few weeks later, Missy returned home from a normal night of patient visits. As the early morning sun filled her house, she wandered into the garage. It was too quiet in there. And it felt empty, despite all the junk that filled it. She looked at the pile of boxes with the folded blankets on top where Ronnie had slept. Her tablet still sat on a box nearby where he had watched videos. Even the scattered iguana bones he had failed to clean up added to her sense of loss.

She missed Ronnie and the brief glimpse of the world of dragons that he had given her.

After putting the blankets in the washer and sweeping up the iguana bones, she caught the scent of ripe mangoes coming in an open window from her backyard tree. She went outside to pick some and dispose of the damaged fruits that had fallen to the ground.

One of the tree's branches was quivering, as if squirrels were on it. Very heavy squirrels.

"Ronnie?" she asked hopefully.

His head appeared from out of the leaves, his jaw chewing, his snout dripping with mango juice.

"Hello," he said. "I sensed you were thinking of me and I dropped by for a quick visit. But there's a lot of ripe fruit on your tree."

She laughed. "As long as you finish the fruit you bite into. It drives me crazy when the birds peck a few holes in one before moving on to another."

He jumped down from the branch, leaving it bouncing. There was no tape holding down his wing anymore. It looked healthy and was folded back properly on his back.

"You're healed!"

He crouched, leaped into the air, then his wings unfolded in their true glory, flapping powerfully and propelling him around the yard. They were so much bigger than she'd thought when they were folded.

Not too high, she told him telepathically. *We don't want anyone to see you.*

There's an iguana in your neighbor's yard.

Nope. No hunting during the day.

He came down for a landing, leaning backwards and beating his wings until he dropped lightly upon his four feet.

"I wanted to thank you for caring for me. And for risking your life to protect me from Moloch," Ronnie said.

"You don't need to thank me."

"Someday we might need your help again."

"Okay, but I hope not," Missy said. "Your mother said it would be a very long time before Moloch came back, if ever."

"Probably not within your lifetime. But there are other evil entities we must be on guard against. My mother is teaching me the dragon magick I need to control the gateway like the adult dragons can. The more of us guarding it, the safer we will be. And having a witch on our side definitely helps!"

"You know where to find me. Keep me informed as the prophesies about you come true."

"I will," Ronnie said, crouching, readying to spring into flight. "I have to go before the gateway moves too far away. Sorry, I'll have to fly over the neighborhood, but I'll be fast. No one will notice."

He took off at an almost vertical trajectory, then headed east. High in the sky with his tail trailing in a straight line, he could be mistaken for a large bird like a Great Blue Heron. Soon, he disappeared into the sun.

Goodbye, Missy. Until we meet again.

Stay safe, she said, wiping a tear from her cheek.

THE END

AFTERWORD

GET A FREE E-BOOK

Sign up for my newsletter and get *Hangry as Hell*, a Freaky Florida novella, for free. It's available exclusively for members of my mailing list. If you join, you'll get news, fun articles, and lots of free book promotions, delivered only a couple of times a month. No spam at all, and you can unsubscribe at any time.

Sign up at wardparker.com.

ENJOY THIS BOOK? PLEASE LEAVE A REVIEW

In the Amazon universe, the number of reviews readers leave can make or break a book. I would be very grateful if you could spend just a few minutes and write a fair and honest review. It can be as short or long as you wish. Just search for "Invasive Species Ward Parker" on Amazon.com and click the link to leave a review. Thank you so much!

COMING NEXT IN FREAKY FLORIDA

Book 3, *Fate Is a Witch*

Embrace your destiny. Even if it kills you.

Missy, nurse to elderly supernaturals, has a passion for witchcraft. And she has two mysteries to solve. First, who is making a series of escalating magick attacks against her that appear to be tests of her growing witchy abilities? If she fails the tests, she dies. If she passes, does that mean she was destined to become a powerful witch?

At the same time, she tries to help cute reporter Matt solve the mystery of who is stealing corpses from funeral homes in Jellyfish Beach, Florida. The embalmer who was about to spill the beans is murdered. And the condition of his corpse suggests a wolf was responsible. There are no wolves in Jellyfish Beach. But Missy knows there are werewolves. In fact, some of them are her patients.

Missy's late parents, whom she never knew, were rumored to have been witches. She wishes she had their guidance. But she does have plenty of unsolicited advice from the Fates. The three ancient Greek goddesses happen to live in a trailer park nearby. They know whether she'll survive or not, but that's the one thing they're not saying. Get *Fate Is a Witch* at ward-parker.com.

OTHER BOOKS IN FREAKY FLORIDA

Did you read Book 1 of Freaky Florida, *Snowbirds of Prey*?

Retirement is deadly.

Centuries-old vampires who play pickleball. Werewolves who surf naked beneath the full moon. A beginner witch who accidentally casts a laxative spell instead of protection spell. You'll meet them and a lot more in Snowbirds of Prey, the first novel of Freaky Florida.

The vampires' survival depends on keeping their supernatural identities secret, but a serial killer has been depositing bodies drained of blood near Squid Tower where they live. Can Missy, the beginner witch, find the real killer before the vampires get staked? Get *Snowbirds of Prey* at wardparker.com.

ABOUT THE AUTHOR

Ward is a Florida native and author of the Freaky Florida series, a romp through the Sunshine State with witches, vampires, werewolves, dragons, and other bizarre, mythical creatures such as #FloridaMan. He also pens the Zeke Adams Series of noir mysteries and The Teratologist Series of historical supernatural thrillers. Connect with him on Twitter (@wardparker), Facebook (wardparkerauthor), Goodreads, or wardparker.com.

ALSO BY WARD PARKER

The Zeke Adams Florida-noir mystery series. You can buy *Pariah* at wardparker.com.

The Teratologist series of historical paranormal thrillers. Get the first novel at wardparker.com.

"Gods and Reptiles," a Lovecraftian short story. Buy it at wardparker.com.

"The Power Doctor," an historical witchcraft short story. Get it at wardparker.com.